DEDICATION

For my Grandma Baker, in honor of hers, the most tender of hearts.
This novel was inspired by my great-great-grandmother, a woman forced to
give up her children because she had no power over her own life.

It broke my grandmother's heart to know how she must have suffered.

unto

Swine

Shannon Stewart

ACKNOWLEDGMENTS

Mrs. Erwin, Grandma Baker, my amazing friends, and my writing workshop mates.

Thank you.

CHAPTER 1

I babysit the little boy they found on the steps of the fire station eight years ago. It was March when the firemen found him, springtime, but still chilly at night. Thankfully they heard him crying right away.

Everyone in Oak Grove still thinks of him as the Fire Station Baby. I hear people talking when they see him out in public, like at the grocery store, or Dairy Queen. They say, "Oh look, there's that, what was it again? Jason? No. Jathan? You know, the Fire Station Baby."

They retell the story as if it happened just the other day. As if anyone in town will ever forget his picture in the Tribute, which came out days after the story broke in the gossip circles.

He's in elementary school now, but he's still the whole town's baby. When people saw him walking and talking like a normal kid, they acted like he was some kind of miracle, evidence of God's own favor on the good people of Oak Grove.

I almost felt sorry for Sheila and Kevin Miller after they adopted him, all those yellowed eyes watching their every move over lowered bifocals. I'm not sure the Millers realized women like Mary Ann Sanders and Mrs. Evans were in a tizzy because Jathan was still on the bottle at 18 months.

If the town ladies ever said anything to Sheila's face, they would have wrapped it in fake concern, or a backhanded compliment like, "Oh I'm so glad his baby teeth are coming in straight and strong. You know, some children would have developed an overbite or milk rot by now."

Sheila isn't bright enough to read between the lines. But I am. They say all kinds of things behind Sheila's back. Once I heard Mrs. Evans and Mrs. Wood in the hallway at school going on and on about how Sheila Miller went back to work when Jathan was two. "Why adopt if you aren't going to raise the child yourself?"

I know they've wrung out their exasperation, and they're about to move on to someone else's problems when they suck their teeth and say, "Well, you know, she's not from around here."

To be honest, I thought he was too young for daycare. And after I learned what milk rot is, I was worried about his baby teeth too. On top of that, I really hated his stupid haircut when he was in kindergarten. He looked like a dork. "Unfortunate," as the town ladies might say.

I kept up with him through the gossip, even after I worked my way into being his babysitter. I don't worry about him so much anymore. He is smart and healthy. He's going to turn out just fine.

I have never thought of him as the Fire Station Baby.

I hear Sheila's footsteps down the hall. Her prancy little tromping grates on my nerves. What a waste of energy, so much bouncing and so little forward progress. It's not her fault that I hate her. She hasn't done anything to me. And she's a good mother to Jathan, as much as she can be, having the soul of a parakeet and all. She's just so completely wrong.

I put my own book aside and sit up on Jathan's bed. He has his elbow on his desk, and he's holding his head by the cow-licked hair above his forehead. He's so focused on the story he doesn't notice when Sheila comes into the room. It startles him, just a little, when she says his name. He blinks a few times, wrenching himself out of the fantastic world in the pages of his book, back to the here and now.

"Hey, mom," he says to her, slow at first, and then a question rushes out of him. "Can I pack my own lunch for the field trip tomorrow? The lunches they send from the school cafeteria are just…" he squishes his eight-year-old face up, "bleh."

I didn't know about this question. It must have been on his mind all afternoon, but he didn't ask me.

"Don't we have some of those Lunchables in the fridge?" Sheila asks. "You could take one of those."

"That's not enough food for a sack lunch," I say. "You should take a peanut butter sandwich. And an apple too."

Jathan nods. I'm his babysitter. He's used to me telling him what to do.

Sheila squints at me, and I think about saying "or whatever" to add some teenage nonchalance, like I'm not actually worried. But then I think about Jathan on a field trip tomorrow, hiking the rocky hills around the lake with nothing but a Lunchable to eat. I ignore her.

"Why don't I help you get it all packed up before I go home?" I'm stuffing my own books into my backpack.

"Why don't you finish your homework, Jathan?" Sheila says, not taking her eyes off me. "I'll pack your lunch. Jade can go on home and finish her homework there."

"Thank you, Mrs. Miller." I smile at her, full wattage. That works on her. The wrinkle between her eyebrows smooths over, and she smiles back at me.

She isn't bright. She hates conflict. To her I'm just an irritating teenager who's nice to her son. That makes it easier, in some ways.

I leave his room, and I can hear Sheila asking about his day. He already spilled it all to me. He laughed so hard he snorted when he told me about playing dodgeball at recess. I laughed too.

I know from experience that a kid who has fun playing dodgeball must be at the top of the heap on the playground. To me, that means there are no bullies making his life miserable at school. He doesn't need me to save him from anything. Not even Sheila. That is such a relief.

I leave their carpeted, air-conditioned house and walk out into the fall heat like stepping into an oven. Sweat is beading up under my shirt by the time I get to the curb. When I pass the convenience store and cross the highway, I can feel trickles running down my back.

On our private road, chunks of crumbling pavement stand out from the dirt like giant rocks. They make the road even worse for driving. But there aren't any cars driving down our road anyway. Only Aunt Rita has a car, and it's broken down again.

I always walk in the middle of the road, as far away from the tall weeds on either side as possible. The last thing I need is to step on a snake. Or get chiggers.

At the end of the fence line, I find the break in the cedar where there's a dirt path. This is our shortcut around the last leaning fence post. It's wrapped in what's left of the tangled, rusty barbed wire that used to keep cows on the property.

On the other side of the overgrown cedar, the farmhouse is just a gray heap of boards in the rough shape of a house, like a pencil drawing. It's full of snakes and skunks and whatever else wants to make a den there. I take the path around it to the back.

I don't know when Aunt Rita moved her trailer back here. I don't even know where Dad got our camper. They've been here as long as I can remember. I do know that the Grandma's single-wide was parked here after she and Grandpa got married. She talks about it sometimes.

I guess mobile homes were a neat idea for a broke couple coming home from Arizona because a job turned out to be a bust. That must have been the seventies judging by the orange shag carpet and green appliances.

Back then, Grandma's parents lived in the farmhouse. That seems impossible to believe now, but I'm fascinated with the idea.

I used to play inside the farmhouse with my cousins when we were little. And at night, sleeping in Aunt Rita's trailer house, I'd fall asleep imagining ways to fix that house so I could live in it by myself. I might have tried to clean it out or nail up some loose boards, I was that obsessed. But in all my imaginings, I couldn't figure out what to do about the gaping hole in the roof.

If that house hadn't been so close, I might not have spent so much time wondering what it would be like to live in one. What a luxury to have a whole room as a kitchen, and a whole other room as a den, and a totally separate room to sleep in. Even when I stayed with Aunt Rita in her trailer, I never had a bedroom. I slept on her fold-out after Momma was gone.

Then Dad got out of the pen, and we moved back into the camper. Now I sleep on the built-in couch against the wall, and he sleeps in the bunk up on the top.

I can smell Dad when I open the door of the camper. He's sleeping with his mouth open, and his stale cigarette breath fills the whole place. I'd leave the door open to let the smell out, but he turned the AC on high again, and I hate to lose the expensive cold air. I close the door behind me as gently as I can. I step so softly the camper doesn't even shake. But he wakes up when I turn off the AC.

"Don't touch that fucking knob! It's hot as hell in here." His voice is full of gravel.

I ignore him and flip the knob down to the low setting, letting my hand hover there until he lowers his head. He's willing to compromise. I don't know how he thinks we'll pay the electric bill. We just got the lights turned back on, and I still don't know where he got the money. But I don't ask those questions.

I look around the camper. It's not dirty. He hasn't done anything but fill an ashtray since he got home last night. There isn't anything to cook, so the tiny sink is still empty. I put my bag in the corner and quietly step back toward the door.

As soon as I turn the handle he speaks. "Where you goin'?"

"Gonna see if Colby's home," I answer. I wait.

"Aight," he finally mumbles. Then he's falling asleep again.

I'm not trying to be quiet now. I tromp down the folding steps and slam the door hard to be sure it latches. The hot air is a relief after his smell.

I bang on Colby's bedroom window as I come around. The threadbare bed sheet in his window moves and I know he sees me.

I knock on the front door, then pull it open before anyone answers. Aunt Rita has cinder blocks in front of her door, stacked in the shape of stairs. I can hear them scrape together under my feet as I climb them.

It's dark in Aunt Rita's house. There's tinfoil on the living room windows. Besides the TV, the only light comes from the water spotted window over the sink.

She's in her usual place in her recliner. On the TV tray beside her is an extra-large plastic tumbler full of Dr. Pepper, and a thin trail of smoke streams up from the satin filtered Virginia Slim in the ashtray.

I don't say anything to her. The TV is too loud, and she'd be bothered by the interruption anyway. I slide past, trying not to block her view as I head for Colby's room. I hear the twins, Bobby and Britney, playing a video game as I pass their closed door in the hall.

My cousin Colby is three years older than me. His little sister, Shelby, is actually closer to my age. She just turned fifteen, and I'm already fourteen. But it's an understatement to say Shelby and I don't get along. Shelby's loud and busy, and always pissed off about what everyone else is doing. Her eyes are black rings of eyeliner around faded blue irises. She cakes makeup over her zits and wears too-short cut-offs made out of pants she outgrew in eighth grade.

Maybe I turned out so quiet because of all the time I spent living with Aunt Rita. I did my best not to set Shelby off. It wasn't that she was tough or anything. She's short and pudgy and has never been hit, not once in her life.

When I lived with Rita, Shelby tried to steal my best pair of pants. I caught her trying them on in the bathroom. We ended up in a hair pulling match on the ground in the hallway. I got her down, and I was about to punch her right in the mouth when Aunt Rita got off the couch to break us up.

Aunt Rita threatened to throw me out of her house over that. Dad was still in prison then. So, I made up with Shelby. I gave her those pants, even though I only had one other pair.

Right after that I got myself a babysitting job, bought another pair of pants when I had the money saved, and learned to steer clear of Shelby.

Right now, Colby is sitting in front of his computer, and thankfully, Shelby isn't home. He's working on an English assignment, and I can tell he doesn't want to talk.

I flop down on the bottom bunk and leave him alone. Silence is comfortable with Colby. And I'm not going back to the camper until it's time to go to sleep.

Colby and I catch a lot of flak at home because we always have our nose in a book. And then we catch a lot of flak from people at school because we live out on the "Jennings' Compound" like a bunch of welfare hillbillies. The only person in the whole universe who actually gets me is Colby.

And even so, there are things I can't tell him.

CHAPTER 2

I like Mrs. Patterson well enough, I guess. I just don't understand why she's so nice to me. She's old and powdery and all fluttery in that ridiculous feminine way that's just so impractical. I'm amazed anyone can keep that up for any length of time. I catch myself thinking about things like this when she comes at me with her questions. How can anyone spend so much effort on something of so little real value?

I first met her when she came down from the high school to help the eighth graders pick their classes. When I sat down at her table in the library, she put her hand over mine, looked right at me and asked me how I was doing.

It was weird. Her hand was cool and light and dry, and I don't think I have ever had a grown person look at me so intently. And then she waited for me to answer, which was unsettling all by itself.

I couldn't think of anything to say. How would I know how I'm doing? I searched the papers between us, the ones with my placement test scores and the previous years' schedules showing all the honors classes I've taken. I was thinking, *Can't you tell how I'm doing from all this?*

"I mean you, sweetie," she said. "How are *you* doing?"

"Oooh," I said, pretending to finally understand. "I'm just fine, Ma'am. Thank you for asking." And I smiled for good measure.

Seriously? Who gives a shit how I'm doing? What a stupid question.

So she put together my schedule, and I chalked it up to some weird old lady situation, until I saw her again at the high school. I swear, when she saw me walking by, she stopped a conversation with another adult and *walked* over to me. She didn't just call out. She stopped me and asked me how I liked high school. Then she wanted to know how I liked my classes. And what lunch I had. And so on and so forth.

I've finally gotten used to this from her, but I still don't understand it. It would help if just once she'd interrogate Colby, or if I happened to catch her checking up on someone else. But apparently, it's just me.

She's tall and that hairdo of hers adds at least another four inches. Usually I see her over the crowd, and I go the other way. But every so often she'll come up behind me or come around a corner.

Like today. She's standing in front of me, and I'm trying to keep my eyes on her face. But I keep looking down the hall, where Mr. Landry is taking attendance as students walk into his class. I shift from foot to foot.

"So, I understand you have a little after school job," Mrs. Patterson starts, and I don't know if it's because she skipped the usual "How are you?" routine, or if it's my own paranoia. I can't help but panic a little. There's no way she knows. That knowledge died with my mother, hanging from a belt in the closet of a cheap motel.

"Yes ma'am." I stare past her to Mr. Landry, hoping she'll get the hint.

"So, you must know the Miller family fairly well then?"

"Yes ma'am." I drag my eyes back to her face and, probably for the first time since I've met her, I look her in the eye. "I've been babysitting Jathan for a couple of years now."

"So how did you come to meet the Millers?"

"I really don't remember, Mrs. Patterson. I think I ran into them at the grocery store or something."

I do in fact remember exactly how I met them. I planned it so carefully. But I'm convincing. Probably because I don't believe I'm lying. What happened in my own mind isn't a matter of truth or lies, is it? Because outside of the watching and waiting and planning in my own mind, meeting the Millers was a complete coincidence.

"Well, it sounds like the perfect job for you," she says. And before I can process what she might mean, she's stepping aside, letting me get to class.

So, this afternoon, I'm sitting with Jathan while he plays his video game, and I replay that conversation over in my mind. There is no way Mrs. Patterson knows anything about what happened. At least nothing that hasn't been through the town gossip ring, and in some cases the newspaper, a jillion times. But I'm still leery. I need my job. Oak Grove is a small town, and there's something about powdery old ladies. They just have to butt their noses into other people's business. And in Oak Grove, that never ends well for a Jennings.

Oak Grove is small enough that the degrees of separation are few, for the most part. The Millers are relatively new, at least by Jennings family standards. We've been here for generations. The Millers got here in the late nineties. Mr. Miller, Kevin is his first name, got transferred here to be the manager of Wal-Mart. Sheila got a job doing something at the State Farm office just off the square.

They're old parents too, by Jennings family standards. I think my Aunt Rita dropped out of high school to have Colby. And Dad was twenty when I was born. The Millers must have been pushing thirty when they decided to have a kid. And way past thirty when they finally got Jathan.

But Mrs. Patterson has been around this town forever. Of course, she doesn't actually live in town. Only people who don't know any better, like the Millers, live in town. Everyone else, the old money in Oak Grove, they all live in big houses on big tracts of land off of farm-to-market roads where you would never suspect money was hiding. And I suppose Mrs. Patterson lives out on a hill somewhere. She probably doesn't lock her doors or have curtains on her back windows. There's probably a miniature lake on her property that she can see from her kitchen table. At least that's how I imagine it.

I guess Mrs. Patterson could know things about my family I don't even know. She was probably at the high school when my parents met. She was definitely there when Aunt Rita got knocked up. I hate to admit it, but Dad has a point when he says public schools are just a way for the government to interfere in private family business.

It's hard to think of Mrs. Patterson as a government agent. But I can't figure her out. She might be just another nosy busy body looking for more gossip to spread around town. But then why isn't she up in Shelby's face with her questions? If anyone could use an intervention, it's Shelby.

In some ways it's good that the Millers are so new. They don't know the stories, the history. They didn't inherit the grudges and the judgment. Someone in town might have told them the Jennings aren't the best family, but how would Sheila Miller know what that really means? What would she know about the kinds of things that happen in a family like ours? Honestly, I think her parakeet brain would shut down completely if she ever had to deal with someone like Dad.

I get on her nerves sometimes, but Sheila doesn't look down on me, or right through me like other people in town do. Mary Ann Sanders told Sheila to lock up her valuables if she was going to have a Jennings in her house. I know because Mary Ann also repeated that to everyone else in town. Shelby couldn't wait to tell me all about it.

Sheila didn't listen to any of them, and that makes me feel even more guilty for hating her. I need Sheila. For many many reasons. I need the money from the job. And of course, I want to prove them all wrong. And there are things I learn about life while I'm at the Miller's house. Stupid things that normal people who didn't grow up in a camper trailer take for granted. Like how to organize your pantry, when to use your good dishes, or how important it is to the neighborhood that you keep your lawn mowed. I'm going to need to know these things for the life I will have some day.

15

I guess these are things your mother should teach you. The closest thing I have to a mother is Aunt Rita, and I'm pretty sure Aunt Rita still doesn't know any of these things.

I mean, I learned things from my own mother, but they aren't concrete things. As much as I understand practicality, the most important things are not practical. They are the fragile things of the heart and soul. I inherited those from my mother before they died with her.

I know with absolute certainty that Sheila is soulless. Not in a malicious way. Not like she's going to kill someone or hatch an evil plot. But just in the way that she doesn't like music, which is bizarre to me. And she reads those novels with the prefab plots. The same story over and over again. It's weird. So, I can't help it, no matter how hard I try not to, I still hate Sheila.

But there is Jathan. Jathan can't miss out on those fragile things of the heart and soul. I have to pass them on to him too.

I look over at him, and he's sprawled over his gaming chair, with his mouth open as he stares at the screen. He's so confident. I can't imagine what that feels like to be so comfortable just being himself. But he is, and I'm glad.

"Jade let's play two player," he says to me. I hate playing video games, but I do it for him. Sitting and watching him play is entertaining enough for me, but I don't want him to think of me as part of the furniture. I want to matter.

So, I pick up the controller. He laughs at me because I keep getting the stupid buttons confused. And when my player gets stuck, and I can't figure out how to make him jump to the right platform, Jathan takes my controller. He gets me over the hard parts, so he doesn't have to leave me behind. When we beat the level, and the screen comes up with our scores, I don't even look. I just take a second to run my hand over that crazy red cowlick and then kiss him on the forehead.

CHAPTER 3

Sometimes I think I might be able to ask Mrs. Patterson about my mother. I mean Mrs. Patterson is always right *there*, with the questions. And my mother wasn't always a Jennings. Honestly, I wouldn't say she ever was.

I think Aunt Rita always hated my mother. But I don't know why I think that. How could you know, when Aunt Rita is so harsh and ticked off all the time, even with her own kids? And I think Grandma must have looked at my mother the same way she looks at me, with this horrible mix of ridicule, pity and disdain.

I miss my mother. Every single day. All day long.

And sometimes, I'll start feeling sorry for myself and get mad at her for leaving me here. It's just a white-hot flash of anger that comes over me every now and then, and I squash it as fast as I can. Because I don't know what made my mother think the Jennings were her only option. I just know that it must have been bad. And then I hurt for her all over again, and I remember what she told me before I went to sleep that last night in the motel.

"You are so much stronger than I ever was."

I was six. Logically I understand she was mentally ill. There is no way a six-year-old can be strong. No way my mother could actually mean that. But once she said it, I was instantly determined to make it true.

I've thought of a million questions I would like to ask Mrs. Patterson about my mother. But I *am* a Jennings. And we just don't go inviting that kind of trouble.

"That book seems to be well below your reading level," Mrs. Patterson says to me, and I look up from *Ink Heart*. I'm sitting outside on a bench in the sun waiting for lunch to be over. I've already eaten my free meal and escaped the echo chamber of a cafeteria for the silence of the courtyard.

"Jathan was reading it…" I say. Actually, he's still reading it. We're reading it at the same time. I got this copy from the public library on the square, and I'm keeping pace with him so we can talk about what's happening in the story.

God help me, there is an entire six minutes left before the bell, and she sits down beside me. She doesn't seem to have anything to talk to me about. She sits quietly beside me for a few seconds while my mind races. I don't know how to do small talk.

Finally, she says, "This is a great spot for reading. And it sure has cooled off, hasn't it?"

My sigh of relief is so strong it sounds like a huff.

"Yes, ma'am. Fall is the best." This is me telling the truth.

"Do you always read the books that Jathan reads?" she asks.

"Just the really good ones," I say.

I suddenly have this feeling that it would be nice to talk to someone about Jathan. But Mrs. Patterson is not that person.

"If he really likes one, he'll start telling me all about it..." I trail off, remembering again that Mrs. Patterson is not that person.

"I bet Mrs. Miller appreciates how much interest you take in him," she says, and leans back against the brick wall behind the bench, settling in.

"I guess."

I close the book and slip it into my backpack, because I can tell I'm not going to get to read anymore.

And then there's a longer silence.

"Mrs. Patterson, did you know my mother or something? I mean why..." I realize what I'm saying. I cannot believe what has just come out of my mouth.

Thank goodness I already have my bag packed, because it's so easy to grab it and jump up from the bench. But even as I stand, I feel her hand on my arm, and I know I'm not going anywhere. Where is there to go? My classroom is still full of students with first lunch.

"Jade," she says, and her hold on me is firm. "Sit down."

I do what I'm told, and then I stare at the white knees of my blue jeans. It's so weird because I'm out of breath, and I don't know why. All I can think is that she's going to diagnose me with something, emotionally disturbed, or some such crap. Then I'll never have a chance.

"Yes, I remember your mother," she says. I realize I'm straining, very slightly, against her hold on my arm. I make myself relax.

"Is that why you follow me around up here?" I ask.

"That's why I'm concerned about you, yes."

"Well, I'm fine," I say. "No need for concern."

"I'm glad you're fine," she says and smiles at me.

I guess I've never really looked at her before, but I see her now. I look at her face, all wrinkled, with freckly spots showing through the powder. She's just a person behind all of that. She's just waiting for me.

"I guessed it was something to do with my mother, because you never ask Colby or Shelby anything. But you knew Aunt Rita too, right?"

"I did know Rita. But your mother was very special to me."

The bell rings, and now I sort of wish I didn't have anywhere to go. But I do. I stand up, and so does Mrs. Patterson.

I don't know what to say. Here's this woman with all these kids to care about, for all these years. And my mother was special to her. That's really enough for me. I need to believe my mother was special to someone.

It's like I'm possessed or something because I hug this tall powdery old woman, right there in the courtyard, in front of anyone who cares to see. Then I turn around and practically run to my class. I blink and blink until my eyes stop burning.

I work even harder to avoid Mrs. Patterson after that. I don't know what came over me, but that can't happen again.

I'm sitting in class after second lunch, and I hear these girls talking about the fight at first lunch. That's how I find out. And it's not like they're going to give me an office pass to go see if Colby's okay.

The girls are laughing about how the fight started, how someone knocked Colby's binder into the giant trash can in the cafeteria. Of course, it was Wyatt and his friend Jordan. And even the laughing girls know Wyatt is a freaking moron. And Jordan is an even bigger moron for being Wyatt's faithful follower. But Colby is one of those kinds of kids, a Jennings kid. So this fight is just a funny story to them, about people who don't matter.

"When he went to get it out of the trash, Wyatt knocked it out of his hands back into the trashcan," I hear a girl whispering behind me.

"Seriously?" a guy's voice whispers back.

"Then Jordan dumped his lunch tray on top of it," a different girl whispers.

"Oh shit! You're kidding!" I guess the guy's voice is still technically a whisper, but he's so loud Mrs. Sanchez looks up and clears her throat.

They stop talking for a few minutes, then the excitement gets the better of them. "So that kid didn't even touch his binder, he just punched Wyatt right in the face."

The other girl chimes in again, "He would have gotten Wyatt good, but Jordan jumped in and started kicking him."

I can't help it. I suck air in so loud the whole class can hear it. I turn around to look at them, and I can see it on their face when they realize I'm listening.

The girl right behind me says, "I'm so sorry. I didn't realize…"

"Is he okay?" I ask over my shoulder. "Did they hurt him?" I'm not even trying to whisper. I don't care what Mrs. Sanchez does to me now.

The girl has to think about it I guess, because she takes forever to answer. She looks like she's scared of me, and I don't really care. I just need to know the answer to the question. So, I ask it again. Louder this time.

She stammers a little then finally says, "Uh, no I think they broke it up pretty quick. And he walked to the office so…"

I let out my breath and turn around. Mrs. Sanchez is watching us, and she knows exactly what's going on. She's looking all snotty and put out with me, with that "Are you done?" look on her face.

I don't want to skip class. I don't want to get in trouble. I want to get out

24

of high school clean. But I need to know what's going on with Colby. After the bell rings, it's my feet that take me down to the office when my mind knows I should be going to my next class.

Jordan's in the chair by the door so the principal's secretary can watch him. I can see through the window in the principal's door. Wyatt is having his turn with the big man. I don't want to walk in. I keep thinking about them knocking Colby's binder out of his hands. The hate feels like acid rising up inside me or something. I don't want to walk in, but I can't see Colby.

I've never been in this office. I don't know anything about the principal's secretary. She looks up at me as I pull the door open, and I expect to be in trouble. So I'm not prepared when she nods at me, like she called for me or something.

"He's in Mrs. Patterson's office, hun," she says to me. "Let me get you a note."

I walk past Jordan to her desk, like it's the most natural thing in the world. I watch her write on one of those little yellow pieces of paper. Just the color of the paper says you require no explanation if you're seen in the halls during class.

I'm so completely unprepared for this kindness, and I feel my face wadding up. I work to keep it straight, but stupid tears are about to roll out of my eyes.

"Thank you so much," I say as she hands me the paper.

"It's okay, sweetie. He's going to be okay."

Dammit. The tears roll down now, and my face tries to squish in on itself. I can't turn around and let Jordan see this, so I have to stand there for a second. Mrs. Lynn pulls a box of Kleenex from the other side of her monitor and hands the whole thing to me.

"Take this with you. I'll get it back from Mrs. Patterson later."

She says it kind of businesslike and that helps. I take one tissue out to get those escaped tears off my face, then walk back out into the hall and down to the counselor's offices.

The attendance clerk's desk is in the common area between the two counselors' offices. The nameplate says Ms. Perkowski, but her desk is empty.

I see the Colby's in the chair across from Mrs. Patterson's desk. He's fidgeting with a baggie of melting ice.

I don't knock. I just walk in. Mrs. Patterson looks up and smiles at me softly, like I'm an adult and we're on the same team. Something in me tries to rise to this, to handle this like a grown person.

Colby turns and looks at me, then ducks his head and turns back. He isn't glad to see me, and I don't care. He'll feel henpecked, I know. He'll be mad I'm out of class. I know he's embarrassed. But he'll get over it.

I slide into the chair next to his and look him over. That red splotchiness high on his cheek, climbing up his temple and wrapping around his eye, will turn into a green and blue bruise. It'll probably cover half his face. It's swelling, but it doesn't look mushy. I guess if he actually broke his face, they'd

26

take him to the hospital.

"I'm good," he says right away. "You need to be in class."

I hold up the yellow paper and smile at him, showing off my contraband.

"They let you come down here?" He's just as surprised as I am by this.

"Are you okay?" I ask him. "They said Jordan was kicking you."

Colby shakes his head, mad. "I'm fine," he says.

"Are you going to be in trouble?" I ask him, but I look at Mrs. Patterson, because she'll know the real deal.

"Colby did hit Wyatt first," she says. "And I understand Wyatt's parents want to bring charges against Colby, for assault."

That's bad. I can tell by the look on her face that it's bad. But I don't know what that really means.

"Are they going to arrest him?"

"No, the police have already been here and taken statements. They're going to set a court date, and the judge will decide what needs to be done."

I can almost feel the defeat and frustration coming off Colby. And not because he's mad about getting beat up, even though I'm sure he is. But because, every single day he gets up with a simple goal; to get himself grown and get himself gone from Oak Grove. He just wants to be where he can make his own impressions on people, without being one of those Jennings kids. It's nothing but a miracle he has three smooth years of high school behind him. And now this.

He's glaring at a spot on the carpet. He won't even look at me, but he shakes his head a couple of times, like he's arguing with himself.

I can almost hear the argument. At home, we talk all the time about our life experiment; finding out for sure whether our parents are doing it wrong, or if life really does just hand some people a shit sandwich. I'm sitting here beside him, and I'm so confused.

I still think our parents are doing it wrong. And I know Colby didn't have to hit Wyatt, which means Colby's doing it wrong too. But I'm so sad for Colby. Because the rage that exploded out of him in the cafeteria was just more of that shit sandwich he was handed. The resentment festers in him more. But I understand how he feels because it wears on me too, having to fight so hard for the simplest things like a fair chance.

I can't help it. I'm watching him, and I know we're wondering the same thing. What's the point in trying?

A broken face would be so much less disastrous than a run-in with the law.

"I know it seems like the end of the world," Mrs. Patterson is talking, and I'm trying hard not to be pissed at her. What would she know about what it seems like?

"But I'm going to speak with the city attorney about this," she says.

That gets my attention, and Colby's head snaps up. She might have said she was going to call up Jesus Christ himself. I can't decide if I'm amazed that she's so well connected, or if she's bat-shit crazy for thinking it's even possible.

"I want you two to get yourselves together and then get back to class." She pulls out her magic yellow pad. "Colby, Mr. Sutfon has assigned you in-school suspension, so you'll need to report to Mrs. Perkins' room."

Colby's face instantly closes up again, and he inhales, like he's about to argue. But Mrs. Patterson stops him before he can speak.

"You could have been expelled." She stops writing and nails him with that look she must have learned in teacher school. "You're going to have to trust me on this. If the prosecutor thinks you've paid your dues here, he'll be less likely to make you pay your dues at the courthouse."

Then she looks at me, with that concerned grown-up look. She nods as if to say, "Don't worry, I'll take care of him." I don't think she means for me to know this, but I'm sure she wouldn't be helping him if it weren't for me.

"So I need you both to do exactly what you have been doing. Stay out of trouble, be respectful and don't talk about what happened."

She hands me my new yellow slip. On my way out the door, I look back at Colby as he takes his yellow slip. He looks confused and doubtful, and I don't blame him. Our eyes meet as he turns for the door. We silently make our appointment to figure this out once we get home.

CHAPTER 4

Sometimes I think about what life will be like once Colby's gone. He says the one good thing about our parents being poor is that we can get more money to go to college. I'm glad he has that all worked out, because I'll need to know how to do it when my turn comes. But after he leaves, I'll have three years left here with no one.

I used to have my own friends, back in elementary school. Sort of. I mean, Julie Watson taught me how to jump rope and play hopscotch in kindergarten. But I think she just needed someone to push around. I don't think she actually liked me. I'm not sure I liked her either. And hopscotch seemed like the most boring waste of sidewalk chalk ever. I really wanted that colored chalk to myself so I could draw pictures. But Julie Watson looked so disgusted when I told her I'd never heard of hopscotch, it made me think there was something wrong with me. That's why I went along with whatever she wanted, even though hopscotch turned out to be every bit as boring as it looked.

I stopped talking in first grade. It wasn't like I was holding words back or anything. I just didn't have any words in me.

I never got in trouble at school for not talking. I did what I was told. I wrote what I needed to for my homework. No one was very upset about it. I do remember Julie Watson trying to talk to me when I first came back. I remember seeing her face going through all these motions, making words. Her eyebrows went up and down, until they finally got stuck low over her eyes. It was like watching her through murky glass.

At first she stopped in front of me to let me know I could play with her if I wanted to. She was happy to see me. But even through the murky glass I could tell she only missed her pushover sidekick. She was a little put out when I didn't fall right back in line.

She never even asked where I'd been. That might have made some girls mad, that your so-called friend didn't care about what happened to you. But I didn't feel anything about it at all. I didn't feel anything when she got mad. I didn't even feel a flicker of relief when she finally gave up and let me sit in the sun alone.

I don't know what the teachers thought of me then. I didn't even look at them, if I could help it. I guess they talked to Aunt Rita about me. Or maybe they talked to Grandma. I sure knew what Aunt Rita thought, though. I'm surprised I don't have indentions in my jawbone for all the times Aunt Rita grabbed my face and made me look at her, yelling, "Answer me Goddammit."

If Grandma was there, she'd break it up with that slow way she has of being the boss of everyone. She'd drag on her cigarette then exhale and say something like, "I don't know why you're so determined to get her to talk. You're gonna get her goin', and then you're just gonna turn right around and tell her to shut up."

There were times, when Grandma wasn't around, I thought Aunt Rita would wear out her arm spanking me, trying to get me to talk. It hurt, but I couldn't even cry about that.

I think it was spring of second grade, maybe around Easter time, when this weird pulling in my middle surprised me. That pulling was so weird because it was the first actual feeling I'd had in almost a year. It was the sidewalk chalk. I wanted it.

I still didn't have any words to offer up, so I just went over to where Julie Watson was hopping around on one leg and took it. I carried it back to my place in the sun and started my drawing there on the sidewalk. It was blue chalk, and I drew a cloud. I tried to make it look like one I had seen in a book, with intersecting overlapping lines.

Julie Watson had a full on hissy fit because I took that chalk, but she didn't come and take it back. Instead she told the teacher on me. I peeked around that murky glass and met Mrs. Randolph's eyes, wondering if she would take the chalk from me. She looked at me for a long time, like she was sad or something. Then she turned to Julie Watson and told her the chalk was for everyone to use. That was all I wanted to know, that I could keep the chalk. I turned back to my cloud.

When we went back out to recess after lunch, Mrs. Randolph came over to my spot with a whole brand-new box of sidewalk chalk. All the colors were in there, and my name was written on the front in black marker.

I know I should have felt special. I should have been more grateful. I can see that now. But back then, feeling anything would have released a flood that might have drowned me for good. I think the human mind can only see so much reality before it resets itself back to a blank beginning. Then you have to rebuild yourself from the ground up. I was only six, but I didn't want to be rebuilt. Not without my mother. With her gone, everything around me seemed like hard edges and clanging racket. I really liked the quiet inside the blank me.

I think when Mrs. Randolph gave me that chalk, she let me know it was okay to want things for myself. I still hold on to that. Maybe I think it's part of being strong for my mother. I wish she had known that what she wanted mattered.

I might have made friends again after that, but all I wanted was to read and draw and be left alone. And when I felt lonely, I followed Colby around. He was only ten, but he seemed like a grown-up to me. The fifth grade was at the middle school, and every day I waited with Shelby on the corner by the elementary school for him to walk us home.

Shelby always ran off at the first chance, inviting herself to her friends' houses, or going inside to watch TV with Aunt Rita. But I stuck close to Colby, and he never tried to get rid of me. We'd wear ourselves out on the monkey bars at the park, or let the sun set on us while we read our library books in the rope hammock behind our camper. Sometimes I'd just lay on the floor with him, building things out of the Legos he got from the Angel Tree Christmas program when he was in second grade.

We talk about things. Books we like. Teachers we hate. Big plans that started as daydreams.

"Jade, don't you wish we had a house with sidewalks."

"Why?"

"Because we could ride our scooters on the sidewalks."

"Yeah, that would be cool. But do you want a scooter, or a bike? I'd rather have a bike, because we could go further."

"Yeah, and we can keep our bikes in the garage."

"What color do you want your house to be, Colby?"

"I want a brick house."

"Oh yeah! Yeah! Me too." I remember how excited I was right then. It's stupid now. But that was when I realized I could imagine whatever I wanted. And Aunt Rita and Grandma might disapprove, but they couldn't stop what I did in my own mind.

I started drawing my imaginary house after that. I drew it on the backs of all of my worksheets. At first it was a two-dimensional house, all sloppy with bricks made out of crooked lines. Then I figured out perspective. If I had time, I drew each brick with mortar in between. And if I was in a hurry, I might just draw enough brick pattern to give the idea that it was a brick house. Sometimes my house had dormer windows, even though I didn't know what they were called until Mrs. Randolph said she like them.

"Have you been to this house?" she asked me once.

"No," I told her, "It's the house I want to live in when I grow up."

I must have gotten that house out of my system. Eventually I moved on to drawing other things like birds and faces. I'm embarrassed about it now, but I was really good at drawing unicorns. I think Mrs. Randolph got tired of me messing up the backs of all of my worksheets, because she started putting scratch paper in my take-home folder.

Then, later, I found sketch journals at the dollar store. They're not that expensive. Now I keep one in my backpack, so I have one everywhere I go.

I miss seeing Colby between classes while he's in in-school suspension. He goes into that classroom every morning and sits at a boxed-in desk. They bring his class work from his teachers every day. I guess if he needs someone to explain it to him, he's just out of luck. He isn't allowed to talk to anyone all day long.

The first couple of days, I come home from the Millers' house and he's sitting on the step of our camper, waiting for me. He's been alone all day, and he wants someone to talk to.

But a week goes by, and he has less and less to say. Now I come home and find him in his room. He's sprawled out on the bottom bunk with his hands behind his head, staring at the bed slats above him. Those yellow boards are still covered in the crayon scribbles Colby and I made when he got his first set of school supplies for kindergarten. Those scribbles are as familiar to me as my own face. Aunt Rita would probably flip out if she knew they were there.

I nudge him, and he moves over so I can slide onto the bed beside him.

There isn't as much room as there was when we were kids. I have to leave one foot on the ground to keep from rolling off the edge. He pulls one of his arms down for me to put my head on.

We lay there, quiet for a while. When he reaches up to trace a waxy blue curlicue, I break the silence.

"Have you told your mom about the fight yet?"

His hand drops back to his chest, and he heaves a deep tired sigh.

"I don't know what to tell her," he says. "I still don't know what kind of trouble I'm in."

He does know what kind of trouble he's in. At least part of it. It's written all over the letter from the school saying Colby is assigned to in-school suspension. The school's letter doesn't mention Wyatt's parents pressing charges. Maybe that letter will come from the police themselves.

I guess it was wrong to take the school's letter out of the mailbox and keep it from Rita. But it seems like this mess is none of her business. She'll just get involved and start mouthing off to the principal or whoever will listen, and make everything worse. Colby and I both understand this. We understand it so well we never needed to say it out loud.

Still, now that we took that letter it just hangs in the air between us like an invisible time bomb that only Colby and I can see. Every day I come home afraid the school has called Rita.

"Have you talked to Mrs. Patterson again?"

"Yeah, she said that attorney guy is supposed to tell her something by Friday," he says. "I guess he went to school here too. She taught him or something."

"So, is it ISS that's bumming you out, or just waiting to find out what's going to happen?"

"Both." I can tell he doesn't want to talk about it.

"Two more days of waiting. Then once you're off the hook, that last few days of ISS will feel like nothing."

We lay there for a while longer, then he shrugs me off his shoulder.

"I have a ton of reading to do. I missed the lecture in Calculus, so I have to try to figure out how to do these problems on my own."

"I'm sorry Colby," I tell him as he digs through his backpack.

He looks up, so discouraged. The smile he works up for me makes me even more sad for him.

Two more days. All our hope is pinned on Mrs. Patterson, and I have no reason to believe she can do anything to help. Except we need her to.

I go back to the camper. Dad isn't home. Since he got out of prison, it's almost like having my own place. I don't have to live with Aunt Rita, and he's never home. If he does come home, it's usually in the middle of the night and he's still asleep when I leave for school. I stay at the Millers' with Jathan as long as I can. Then when I come home, I hang out with Colby as long as I can. If it all works out, Dad's gone by the time I go to bed.

I wash and fold Dad's clothes and put them in the box next to his bed. I wash the dishes he leaves in the sink and empty his ashtrays. I try to think of anything I can do to keep him happy, so we don't have to talk.

I'm not just scared of him. I think he's a moron. And it's really hard to let a moron boss you around. I'm so afraid I'm going to roll my eyes or look like a smart-ass when he starts trying to be all fatherly. I guess he might hit me or whatever, and that is always bad. But mostly, if I just keep him happy and feeling like he's in charge, then every so often he leaves money for me on the counter next to the sink.

He wants receipts for the electric bill and the groceries. That's not a problem for me. I don't know where he gets the money. Okay, that's a lie. I know he's selling something. And it doesn't matter whether it's weed or meth, he could get thrown back in prison for it. I know how bad that would be for me. But when the money is there on the counter, and I can go buy whatever I want to eat from the corner grocery store, and I don't have to feel like I'm freeloading off of Aunt Rita, I just can't get mad at him about it. As long as I don't have to listen to his shit.

So when I come home on Thursday, and I hear him yelling as I walk up to Aunt Rita's house, I start getting irritated that he's going to be annoying the crap out of me all night. I almost go back to the camper to avoid whatever's going on in Aunt Rita's house, but then I hear Aunt Rita.

"Jimmy! That's enough," she's yelling too. "Let him go."

"Little motherfucker wants to end up in prison? I'll show him what he'll get in prison," Dad says, "You like this?"

I yank open the front door of the trailer, and it takes my eyes a second to adjust to the darkness inside. And then it takes a little bit longer for me to realize what I'm seeing in the light from the door.

Dad has Colby down on his knees, holding him by the back of his hair, and there is a thick stream of blood between Colby's nose and mouth. Aunt Rita is in the corner, on the other side of the coffee table. At first I wonder what she thinks she can do to help from back there, twisting her hands together. She looks up at me like she thinks I can do something. It's like a rolling ball of fire comes up through me when I realize she's back there because she's scared. She's too scared to do anything to help Colby.

That chickenshit loud-mouthed bitch.

Before I even know what's happening, I'm charging for Dad. I hit him in the side before he even knows I'm coming. Colby falls back on his hands and scoots away, trying to get on his feet.

Dad catches his balance and turns to look at me. He looks too stunned to be mad, but I know that won't last. I stand there heaving, braced and waiting for him to realize what just happened and come after me.

He glares at me. And then he moves forward. But he only pushes past me, shoving me sideways as he goes out the front door.

Now the three of us, Aunt Rita, Colby and me, are standing there looking at each other. I glance down at the floor where a few drops of Colby's blood fell onto the matted carpet.

"Get him a goddam washrag!" I yell at Aunt Rita, and I don't give a shit if she does come around that table to smack me.

She blinks a few times and looks at Colby like she's melting, like she wants to hug him or something. Then she looks back at me and goes into the kitchen for a wet rag. She hands it to me and watches while I wipe at Colby's face, trying to see if his nose is broken.

Colby can only handle so much of my awkward wiping before he takes the rag from me and presses it into his nose.

Now I don't know what else to do. I feel myself start to bawl. It comes all at once, and Colby wraps his free arm around me to pull me close. I let it go for a minute, all tears and snot. Then I start to wonder about Dad. Where he went. What he's going to do. And that dries up my tears in a hurry.

I look around the living room. The door is still open, swinging slowly in the breeze that's whistling around the trailer. There's a letter on the coffee table. It's not the one from the school. In the top corner of this letter I can see the city logo, a bunch of oak trees in a circle. The branches form the words Oak Grove. The same picture is next to the city limit sign on the highway.

"They're not bringing charges against me," Colby says before I can even pick up the letter. "She did it."

I know he means Mrs. Patterson. I start to bawl all over again.

Shelby appears in the sunlight and demands to know who left the damn door open, until she comes inside and sees us all looking like someone just died.

"What the hell?" she asks.

"It's nothing baby," Aunt Rita tells her. "It's gonna be alright."

Bobby and Britney push past Shelby and come inside. They run to Aunt Rita who slumps down onto the couch and tries to pull them into her lap. They've been too big to sit in her lap for a while, but how would she know that?

I'm disgusted again. This new outburst of motherly love is sickening. I follow Colby to his room. We just stand there, staring at each other, trying to process what just happened.

She did it.

Dad's in bed when I come back to the camper. I know he's not asleep, but I don't say anything. I'm scared to have my back to him. But I make myself stand at the sink and wash the dirty saucepan he used to warm up a can of chili. I make myself a sandwich. My mouth is dry and the bread is hard to swallow, but I eat it all.

Then I slide myself up to the fold-out table and pull out my Geometry book. I feel trapped sitting at the end of the built-in couch with the table in front of me. But I go through the motions, like there's nothing wrong in the world.

"You know I can't stand that little candy ass," Dad says after a while. "But he wouldn't last a minute in prison. He's such a pussy. Somebody has to teach him."

This is Dad's apology.

"I know," I say, and it feels like a betrayal, like I'm agreeing with him about Colby. I switch off the light and lay down before I start to cry again. Dad has to get his satisfaction, one way or the other. What good would it do to argue?

What I get in exchange for the betrayal is peace. The whole thing is over now.

"I need to thank someone for a huge favor, but I don't know what to do."

Sheila looks all proud and pleased with herself that I'm asking her for advice.

"Well, a card is what most people do. Sometimes a small gift is appropriate," she starts in. I kind of regret asking her because she's so annoying with her know-it-all Miss Manners crap. But it makes her happy, and she probably has some good ideas, so I let her go on. "Or you could make something, maybe bake some cookies. A lot of people say thank you with baked goods."

"Baked goods…" I repeat it just to see how it feels to say it.

Then I laugh to myself. Sheila has her eyebrows up because she has no idea why I think that's funny. Baked goods, who says this crap?

"I can't bake," I tell her.

She smiles, all sympathetic, like it's some kind of disability.

"Well, you're a smart girl. You'll think of something," she says. "And if you want to look through my recipes, I'd be glad to help you bake something simple."

She looks so excited about this possibility that I pretend to be excited about it too. Before I know it I'm following her down the hall, and she's clapping her hands together the way she always does when she's happy. It's embarrassing.

In the kitchen, she pulls out a little wooden box full of index cards with frayed edges. There's a tab with the words "Baked Goods" handwritten on it. Behind that, she flips past a few smaller tabs labeled "Brownies", then "Cakes/Cupcakes" and she gets to "Cookies." She flips some more and pulls out a recipe for sugar cookies.

"This was the first cookie recipe I ever made," she says to me and lays it on the counter.

Now I feel like crap for being so snotty, even if I didn't actually act snotty. I have to think my mother would be grateful to Sheila for this. So when I look at Sheila this time and say "Thank you," I really really mean it.

She runs through the list of ingredients and checks her pantry for the things she already has that I can use.

"I can bring the ingredients," I tell her. "Jathan and I can stop at the store on our way home from school tomorrow."

"Just bring some eggs and milk. It doesn't make sense for you to buy all the other stuff when you won't use that much," she says. "And look for something to carry them in. They have some cute little boxes. I can't remember if they're on the baking aisle or with the Ziploc stuff."

I'm okay with making cookies I guess, but it isn't enough. I need a better way to tell Mrs. Patterson how grateful I really am. Sugar cookies just don't say it all.

I'm lying on the couch, and I can't sleep, so I pull out my sketch journal and start doodling. It's the best way I know to zone out so ideas will come to me. I turn to a blank page, and I start to sketch, kind of small, in the bottom corner.

I'm drawing the prison visiting room where my mother used to take me to see Dad. Except behind the glass in the visiting booth it isn't Dad there, but Colby. My faces aren't that good when they're so small. I make it Colby by adding the Pink Floyd prism from his favorite T-Shirt. It's like my worst fears are coming out onto the page. At first it feels good to get it out of me so at least I can look at it head on. In my mind this is what Mrs. Patterson saved us from. But then I can't stand to look at it anymore, afraid that if I conjure it up on a piece of paper it will set the universe into action, making it real.

So, I keep drawing. In the upper corner I draw that stupid house again, with sidewalks and a garage. And then I draw the Double Ts from the Texas Tech logo between the visiting room and the house. And I add some generic math equations, and draw some books so that they surround the visiting room, blocking it in. In another corner I make the top of a drafting table with a compass and some graph paper on it. Then I draw a skyscraper coming up from behind that table. It's an ordinary skyscraper, and I'm sure Colby would laugh at it, but it's symbolic to me. And I surround the top of that skyscraper with clouds that look like they might have been drawn by a second grader.

It's almost midnight when I quit drawing, and I know I'm going to be tired in the morning. I close my journal and set it on the table, then close my eyes. Right before I fall asleep, I pull out my blue map pencil and flip the journal back open so I can color the clouds powdery blue.

CHAPTER 5

Sheila and I bond over making cookies, I guess. Now I feel like I need to bake her cookies too.

When Jathan comes out of his room all excited at the smell coming from the oven, I can kind of see why people like to bake.

"Do I get some cookies, too?" he asks.

Sheila and I answer at the same time. She says no, and I say yes.

"These are for Jade's teacher," she says.

"She won't miss a few," I tell her and smile. We made two dozen. "They won't all fit in the box."

Jathan is so excited about cookies he abandons his book and hops onto a bar stool. We hang out in the kitchen while we wait for the cookies to bake.

"So, what are we thanking Mrs. Patterson for?" Sheila asks, all smiley, like someone who never needed saving from any kind of trouble in her life.

I come up with my answer fast enough. "She really helped Colby a lot this year, with him trying to go to college and all."

Not a lie.

It hits me how perfect this moment is. I mean, as perfect as it can be without my mother. With Sheila here instead. This perfect house, with cookies baking, with Jathan all happy, safe, and warm. I sit down beside him and lean over to press my nose into his cowlick so I can inhale the smell of his hair. I can get enough. I want to soak it in and keep it forever.

At home, before I go to sleep, I draw the kitchen on a new page in my journal. I even put Sheila in there with us. I wish I could draw the smell of Jathan's hair.

I feel so stupid carrying those cookies to school. The box is polka-dotted, pink and brown. When I picked it out I wanted something Sheila would approve of, not really thinking about how embarrassing it would be to carry the stupid thing around. Colby looks embarrassed too. I just want to get it to Mrs. Patterson's office and get to class as fast as I can.

I walk into the counselors' office and the attendance clerk is there this time. I know her. Mrs. Perkowski. Her first name is Tancy or Tally or something weird like that. That's what sucks about living in a small town. Her husband is the cop that arrested Dad. Not the only cop to arrest Dad, but the one in charge of the bust that sent Dad to prison.

Aunt Rita saw this woman in Wal-Mart once and cussed at her until she popped her daughter up out of the shopping cart and walked away. She wasn't dressed up for work that day, but I'll never forget her. I was about ten maybe. I remember seeing her flip-flops slapping against the bottoms of her feet after she left her grocery cart right there in the aisle, a carton of ice cream sweating on the cans of soup.

The sight of her stops me at the door, and I forget what I'm doing. She smiles at me. For a second I kind of hope she doesn't know who I am.

"Can I help you?" she asks. Her smile shrinks a little, like maybe she can't stand the thought of helping me.

"I need to leave these for Mrs. Patterson," I say, holding up the box.

"You can leave them on her desk," she tells me and cuts her eyes toward Mrs. Patterson's office.

I practically run into Mrs. Patterson's office and set the box down on the corner. I'm about to get out of there when an idea comes to me. I swing my backpack off my shoulder super fast and squat down to pull out my sketch journal. I flip to the page where I drew Colby and his futures. I tug at it, gentle, until it comes loose. Then I tuck the rough edge under the box of cookies. Once I jam my journal back into my book bag, I take off for class without another look at Tally, or Tandy, or whatever her name is.

Done.

I like the feeling when winter hits, but only at first. Like that first morning when you wake up and you can see your breath on the air. It's such a relief from the heat I can't imagine ever getting tired of it. And it does kind of look like a Christmas storybook when they decorate the square, and they dress up those mannequins in the antique shop to look like Santa Claus.

But by the time Christmas actually rolls around, I'm tired of being cold. Dad says there's no insulation in the camper, and the heater can't compete with the drafts. He stays home more in the winter too, and he's enough to make anyone choose to be out in the cold. I want to be anywhere rather than cooped up with him. Sometimes I just stand in the shower, letting warm water run over me, hoping to get thawed out all the way before I have to sleep next to those roll-out windows again.

Afternoons with Jathan are the best. The Millers have their fake tree up next to their fake gas fireplace. There are a ton of presents under it for Jathan, and some of them are from me. I can't afford to buy him video games, but I bought him an Amazon gift card so he can buy books to download to his Kindle. And I bought him a copy of Fablehaven in hard back, just because he loves that book so much.

I wish I could be there when he wakes up on Christmas and opens them, but that's never going to happen. Sheila has taken off work for the two weeks Jathan is out of school. I won't see him until January.

It's the day before Christmas break, and I'm finished with my science lab. I stack my books up on my desk and put my head down to wait for the bell.

When the door opens, I barely notice because there's so much commotion in the room with the other kids still drawing the bacterial growth in their Petri dishes because they never stop talking.

Mr. Landry calls my name, and I raise my head. He holds up a yellow slip. Mrs. Patterson wants to see me.

I'm trying not to be scared. I can't think of a single reason to be scared. Everything is going just fine as far as I can tell. Colby and I haven't caused any trouble. Wyatt hasn't even looked Colby's way since the fight. But my chest still feels tight, like something bad is going to happen.

Mrs. Perkowski must be at lunch when I come in. I pass her desk and look into Mrs. Patterson's office. She's typing something into her laptop, and she doesn't know I'm there.

"Mrs. Patterson?" I say. "You wanted to see me." I hold up the yellow slip.

"Oh Jade, yes." She turns to me and pulls her glasses off her face. "Come in and close the door."

I guess I make a face because she laughs a little. Not a full laugh though, not enough to be comforting.

"It's fine love, I just wanted to share something with you," she says. "A Christmas gift of sorts."

I close the door behind me and edge my way between her desk and the chair where Colby sat the day of his fight. I just hang my rear end on the edge of it. I don't exactly sit in it.

"I wanted to tell you how much I appreciated the cookies," she says. "And the drawing—" She stops herself here, and her eyes get all weird and red, even more wrinkly. I guess that's what old people's eyes look like when they're about to cry.

"Yeah, I'm sorry about that. I know it was stupid. I don't know why I put that under those cookies."

"It was not stupid, Jade. It was beautiful," she says. "And I want to talk to you about why you're not taking any art classes, but we can get to that when you come back from break next semester."

It's a relief when her eyes go back to normal.

"It looks like that drawing came out of a sketch book."

I nod. I can think of no way that this could create a problem for her, much less make her cry.

"I want to give you something that I've held onto for a very long time," she says, and then her eyes get all crinkly and red again. "It was your mother's."

She looks down, and I see her hands are folded over something on her desk in front of her. It's an old-school Trapper Keeper notebook, like from the eighties or nineties. It has hearts and rainbows and clouds all over it. The white plastic has gone yellow in the creases. She pulls the front flap, and the Velcro makes a ripping sound as it comes open. It's crammed full of pages, some lined notebook pages with bubbly cursive handwriting in blue ink. Other pages are bigger and thicker and look like the binder rings were punched through them.

I know immediately that it's my mother's journal. The pages look just like the pages in mine.

"I'm sorry, Ma'am?" I hear myself say. I realize that Mrs. Patterson has been talking, and I have no idea what she's saying.

"I was saying, I always knew I needed to give this to you. I just didn't know when it would be appropriate."

"How do you have this?" I ask her, and I reach out to touch the top page, but then I pull my hand back and look at her.

"I took it," she tells me. "From the camper. After they found her, I went to check on you at Rita's. Before I left, I went inside the camper to see for myself..." She puts her hand up to her mouth, and it looks like she's trying real hard not to cry now. "I thought they might throw it away."

I get the feeling I'm supposed to know what to do here. Like I'm supposed to say something that will make all this better, but I don't have any idea what that would be. I slump back in the chair and sit there, feeling like all the air is gone out of me, and all my thoughts too.

"There were other things in her locker. A sweater, I think. Everything was donated to Goodwill, but I kept this."

She reaches under the pages and pulls out a tiny gold chain that is looped between the rings. A red stone, set in gold, dangles from the chain. It's a ruby.

"I think you're old enough to appreciate this now."

I was old enough to appreciate it when I was six, but I don't say that.

Part of me is mad as hell that she thinks she has the right to decide when I'm ready to get my mother's personal belongings. Part of me is pissed off that she's so judgmental she didn't think I would appreciate this. As if she knows me. As if she knows what my mother means to me.

And part of me knows she was right to take it. Because I might have treasured this memento of my mother's, but I don't know if I could have kept it safe while I was being shuffled around.

I'm scared of what's in those pages. As scared as I've been of anything, ever.

She folds the binder up, presses the flap to mash the Velcro together, and reaches for her yellow pad. She writes my pass to my next class, sticks the slip-on top of the retro notebook and holds the whole thing out to me.

It's too sudden. Too soon. I need more time to get ready. I leave her hanging there for a second while I get up my nerve.

"I'll be right here when school starts back," she says when I reach out. "Make some time for a visit."

CHAPTER 6

I hold the notebook against my chest until I get out of the counselors' offices. I know the bell is about to ring and the halls will be full of obnoxious kids, even more obnoxious when they're happy about Christmas break.

I can barely fit the binder in my backpack. I manage to slide it in front of my Geometry book, then pull the drawstring tight so I can stretch the flap down and close the clasp.

I see it four more times before I leave school, at the beginning and end of my last two classes. I know at some point I'll think about what's inside. But right now, I'm only worried about protecting it. Worried that someone will see it and ask me a stupid question.

I don't go to the elementary school, or to the Millers'. The elementary kids got out of school early, and Sheila picked Jathan up. I'm kind of sad I won't get to see him one last time, but I know he's happy to be a car-rider. He always wants to be a car-rider. At least he doesn't have to walk home with me in the cold.

It's a little weird to get home while the sun is up. The days are so short lately it's getting dark before I make it down the gravel road. The place looks better in the dark. The dark hides the things that drive me crazy, like the stacks of red iron at the end of Rita's trailer. Who knows how long those bars have been laying there or where they came from? Now there are weeds growing up around and in between them, wherever they can squeeze through. I get tired of looking at the weeds too.

My mother planted a garden once. She cleared a spot behind our camper, out and away from the trailers. I barely remember it. I just remember the dark dirt she turned over with the hoe, and how tall the rows seemed when I was little. That patch still stands out from the rest of the rocks and cactus-covered ground. In the summer it grows rye grass so thick and tall it looks like a tiny wheat field blowing in the wind. Now it's just a yellow patch of dead grass.

When I open the camper door, I can tell right away the pilot light is out. I can smell the propane. I leave the door open to let that stinging wind blow away the gas. I open my backpack to get a piece of notebook paper, and there's the binder again. I pull it out and set it on the table where it looks out of place. But I know this binder has been here before. I'm tempted to open it up and flip through the pages, but I need to get the heater going. So, I tear a piece of paper out of my own binder and roll it up tight.

I keep a lighter hidden on the inside ledge of the little access door to the heater. Otherwise, I'd never have a lighter when I need one. Dad has a habit of carrying them off.

The rolled-up notebook paper burns fast. Black pieces of it break off and fly away. The wind blows them toward Rita's and Grandma's houses, but the burnt pieces are nothing but ash by the time they get close. Still, I need to hurry before the flame gets my fingers.

I jam the piece of paper into the small space where the pilot is. It catches fire with a flash then shrinks down to a nub of blue light. I realize I forgot to turn off the thermostat when I hear the furnace light with a deep whoosh. I drop the paper on the ground and watch what's left of it burn away to black ash. Then I go back inside to wait for the heat to do it's best to warm my little box of a house.

I sit down at the table. It's hard to move my arms without letting my blanket fall away from my shoulders. So, I sit and look at the rainbows and clouds, rubbing my hands and arms until they're warm.

I look around one last time before I pull open the flap, just to make sure no one's coming to interrupt me. I hear the tear of the Velcro again and lay the whole thing out flat. On top is a piece of notebook paper covered in handwriting. In the top corner of the page my mother has written her name. And in the other corner is the date, like a homework assignment.

Ruby Bell _____ 9/20/1994

I missed the bus that day, and I didn't want to call Sandy and tell her I needed a ride. She would've been so mad. I remember how my throat hurt as soon as I saw the bus pulling away, like someone was pressing it closed. I started to run, even though I knew the bus wouldn't stop. I just panicked for a minute.

It took me a while to give up on the idea of catching it. But I didn't cry.

Not there in the bus line. I caught myself and looked around. They were all looking at me. I only caught Sherry Randolph's eyes, but I knew the rest of them were watching.

So, I ducked my head and pulled my books against my chest until I could get around the corner. I got past the regular walkers. The ones who live nearby. I tried to swallow, trying to get that rock in my throat to go down. I kept thinking about how it's four miles from the high school to Sandy's house. And I was thinking how the bus usually takes more than an hour to get there because of the stops. I was hoping if I ran some of the way, maybe I could get home before the bus passed in front of the house. Before Sandy noticed I wasn't on it.

I didn't bother looking down at my shoes. They were already fraying along the sides. My pinky toe would be showing through by the time I got home. I could feel blisters forming on my heels. I knew Sandy would be mad again when she found out I needed new shoes. I'd been planning to fix them. Maybe with some duct tape on the inside.

A backpack would have really helped. It might've made running down the road a lot less awkward. That's why I waited to start running until I was past the church on purpose. So, I would be far enough away that the people at Sonic couldn't see me. And still, one of those kids with a car drove by. I couldn't see the driver, but the car slowed down, and I saw the passenger. It was a girl. She pulled the straw out of her mouth and said, "What the fuck?" She didn't yell it at me. She was asking the driver.

I was so embarrassed. I stopped running until the car turned off the highway and drove out of sight. But the whole time I walked, I felt panic creeping up on me because I needed to hurry. So, when the car was gone, I took off running again. Until I felt the skin coming off my heels. And then I only stopped long enough to fold the backs of my shoes down and catch my breath. When I started again, I was so clumsy, running probably wasn't much faster than walking.

I made it all the way to the part of the highway where the shoulder ends. Then I heard gravel crunching under tires behind me. It scared me so bad I think I spun around before I even stopped running. One of my shoes slipped off, and I stumbled back, trying to get my foot back into it. I landed on my hands. Those rocks, the white ones, were so hot and they tore into my palms. I couldn't see over the hood of the car, it was so close. I knew I needed to get up. From the ground, I could see how easy it would be me to get run right over.

The care sort of jumped on its tires, slipping in the gravel too. I crab-crawled backwards. I just knew it was coming for me. But all I managed to do was lose both my shoes, and kick up some dust and rocks. I couldn't get on my feet. Then I saw the driver's side door open. That's when I stopped trying to get away. I knew it meant the car was stopped.

Mrs. Patterson's pointy high heels were all wobbly in the gravel. She held out her hand to me, but I didn't take it. I was too afraid I'd pull her down on top of me. I managed to get myself up without any help. Then I remembered my books. I just knew I was going to be in trouble for dropping them in the dirt.

She wanted to know why I was running down the highway. She asked me if I was in some kind of trouble. I'm sure she thought I was stupid because it took me a minute to understand that she was asking me a question and not yelling at me.

I told her I missed the bus. I was about to explain how it wasn't my fault, even though it really was, but I wasn't doing anything bad. I saw her look down at my feet, and I remembered my shoes. I turned around and tried to get my feet back into them while I was talking, but I wasn't doing a good job at either.

Then I remembered the real trouble I would be in when I got home, and I asked her what time it was. She didn't really know, she guessed it was after four-thirty. She told me she was going to drive me home.

I forgot to blink. I could feel the dust in the air sticking to my eyes. She must have thought I have some kind of brain damage. I couldn't talk, and I couldn't move. I did not want to get in her car. She has a nice maroon one. I could barely hear it, even though it was still running.

Then she was like "Ruby, your hands are bleeding on your books. I'm going to take you home." There was sticky blood on the cover of my geometry book. I told her I'd clean it off. It wasn't on the pages or anything. She said she wasn't worried about the books. But she sounded like she was getting annoyed with me at the same time. But not like yelling at me really. Just like, Ruby quit being stubborn, give me the books and get in the car.

I didn't want to give them to her. I didn't have anything else to hold onto. But I did what she said. I could feel my heartbeat in my hands when I let them go. I knew she wasn't really mad at me, but I'm so stupid, I still jumped a little when she took me by the back of the arm. I guess I was afraid she would yank me around or something. But she only held me steady while I got to the car, and then she opened the door.

The inside of the car was all new and smooth and clean, with glowing lights on the flat buttons. She had the air conditioner on, and there was some elevator music playing on the radio. I was sweaty and dirty, so I put my binder under my feet to keep the dirt off her carpet.

She said, "Please, don't worry about my car," and I know she was trying to be nice. But polite people always say that, and they never mean it. After all, someone has to clean up the mess, right?

Even if I wanted to, I don't think I could have talked while I was in that car. I looked at the buttons on the dash, and the buttons on the doors for the locks and windows. This stupid idea came to me that her car was some kind of a time machine. I mean, I knew it wasn't. But it was just so familiar. And when she pulled out onto the highway, I still couldn't hear it running. When it went over the cattle-guard, it was so smooth, like it was floating. I got dizzy just thinking about how something as simple as a car could feel so weird and familiar at the same time. I kept breathing. Just breathe until it's over. That's what I have to learn to do.

She asked me if I was okay when I leaned my head down and rubbed my eye. It's always the right eye that feels weird. I guess that's where my face hit the window when my parents' car crashed. I told her I was fine, just dizzy. Maybe from running in the heat. She said I might feel better after I got home. But I knew that wasn't true because she was way wrong about the time. It was already after five.

Mrs. Patterson just had to drive me all the way up to the house. I was worried about what the gravel driveway would do to her car. I told her over and over that she didn't have to go to so much trouble. She said she wanted to come by and visit Sandy anyway, but that didn't make me feel any better.

Sandy complains about the monthly visits from the social workers. She doesn't like people in her business, and she really doesn't like that the foster kids all have a psychologist. Sandy almost lost her license when someone's psychologist said Craig felt Jenna up. I don't know if high school counselors count, but I was sure Sandy wasn't going to like Mrs. Patterson just stopping by for a visit.

I got out of the car as fast as I could, hoping Sandy would come and meet Mrs. Patterson outside. If Sandy could hold her at the door, maybe she wouldn't be so mad, and I wouldn't be in as much trouble.

Sandy must have been waiting for me because she was right there by the front door when I opened it. I didn't have a chance to explain to her about Mrs. Patterson before she had me by the arm. The same arm Mrs. Patterson grabbed earlier.

She yanked me into the house, and I almost dropped my books again. She was yelling at me, asking where I'd been. She almost slammed the door in Mrs. Patterson's face, but Mrs. Patterson caught it. Then she smiled at Sandy, like they were good friends. Like she didn't see Sandy's grip on my arm. Like she hadn't heard Sandy yelling at me. And I was really thankful for that.

Sandy let me go, and we moved out of the way so Mrs. Patterson could come in. I started to talk, to smooth it all over, by saying that Mrs. Patterson gave me a ride home. Sandy was smiling back at Mrs. Patterson and saying how nice that was of her and how worried they were about me. She said Craig just left to go look for me.

She used her foster parent voice to tell me that if the library is too busy after school, I just need to get out of line and catch the bus because they only have the one van. And I already know all of these things. She was saying them to me, but she was saying them for Mrs. Patterson to hear. So, I said yes ma'am. I used my good foster kid voice too. I hoped that meant it would all be over. I told her I was really sorry.

Then Mrs. Patterson joined in and said I was such a sweet girl. She said she was going to be keeping tabs on me. Sandy looked surprised by that. She looked at me again, like she wondered what Mrs. Patterson was talking about. Like maybe we weren't all just putting on a show.

Mrs. Patterson asked Sandy about my shoes. I was so embarrassed. She said it looked like I needed new ones and wanted to know what size I wear. She was asking Sandy, but how would Sandy know? There are eight of us foster kids in school, not even counting the two toddlers. I couldn't speak up to answer her. I didn't want to look like a beggar. Even if I wasn't too embarrassed to speak up, Sandy would get mad if I acted like she wasn't taking care of me.

Sandy asked me what size my shoes were. I wish she had asked what size I wear instead. I told her they were sevens. Mrs. Patterson didn't say anything else about the shoes, so who even knows why she asked? She changed the subject.

She said something about how busy Sandy must be with all her foster
kids, with the little ones and all. Sandy said something like "Well it's just
on our hearts to do for these kids who don't have anyone else." Then Mrs.
Patterson said, "Let me know if you need anything."

Then Mrs. Patterson looked at me for a long time. She said my name.
She said it was "an absolutely beautiful name."

I wanted her gone, but at the same time I didn't. I was scared of what
Sandy was going to do.

I don't hear Dad coming. I'm reading so fast, and breathing so hard, he
sneaks up on me, even as loud as he is. The door comes open, and the light
pours in. He fills the door, and then it closes behind him. I can't see his face.
I can't tell what kind of mood he's in except that he doesn't slam the door.
That's a good sign.

I don't think. I close the binder. I want to protect it from him. I should
have been watching out for him.

"What's that?" he asks.

"It's a Trapper Keeper."

"I know it's a fucking Trapper Keeper," he says. I can only see the bottom
half of his face under the bill of his camouflage cap. His lips have
disappeared. They fold in around teeth so small and dark they're hard to see,

even when he speaks.

"It was Momma's," I say, suddenly ready to defend it with my life.

"I know whose it was," he says. "Where the fuck did you get it?"

I don't tell him that Mrs. Patterson gave it to me. I don't want him to know about her.

"The school had it," I say. "It was in the lost and found."

He pulls his cap back, and I can see his small blue eyes. They're like Shelby's without the thick eyeliner. I can see why she wants to add some substance to their watery nothingness. He squints at me and then eyes the notebook.

"They must have fossils up there in that lost and found." He steps forward and thumps the cover. "That piece of crap was already old when she got it."

I sit as still as I can and keep my eyes down. I'm barely breathing. I just know he's going to take it from me.

He stands there, too still for Dad. I make myself look up at him, and he's looking at the notebook. His face is sort of soft. The white skin in the creases around his eyes is showing. As scraggly as he is, he looks like a little kid.

"What's in it?" he asks.

"Nothing," I lie. "Just some old notebook paper."

"Hmmph," he says, and turns to the kitchen drawer. He's back on whatever errand brought him home in the first place, but he still has that look on his face. "I guess it's cool now, to have that old crap?"

I realize I hear a car running outside. Someone's waiting for him. Probably Uncle Ellis or Harmon.

"I made so much fun of her for carrying that stupid looking thing around." He flips through one drawer and then another.

I'm relieved. I don't think he's going to take the notebook. But I can feel my face get hot when he says "her." I can't remember the last time he mentioned "her."

"I had a whole carton of cigarettes," he says and looks at me. He's back to being squinty.

"You smoked them," I say. "You were down to one pack, so I threw the box away and put the last one on the shelf over the sink."

He eyes me again, his truth test.

"I don't smoke," I say.

He glares at me as he leaves. "You better watch that smart mouth," he says over his shoulder as he walks out the door, but I know he isn't really mad.

CHAPTER 7

Sandy didn't yell at me or give me any more chores. I expected to get potty chair duty again. But she was nice to me after Mrs. Patterson left. So nice she made me a little nervous at first. But it's amazing how easy it is to get used to things. She even let me go with her to the grocery store on Saturday. I didn't really want to go. I didn't feel right being alone with her for so long. I didn't know what we would talk about on the trip there and back. But I didn't want her to stop being nice to me, so I went.

Now Carrie is giving me the cold shoulder. Every time I come into our room she cuts her eyes at me. I keep asking her what's wrong, but she just says, "nothing." In the morning, all the other girls stop talking as soon as I come into the kitchen. Even the little girls stop and look at me like I have something wrong with me. Even Caroline.

I know it's because Sandy treats me like her favorite. I know because when Jenna was here, and she made friends with Sandy, the other girls were so mean to her. Most of those girls are gone now. All of them except Carrie and me.

Carrie started the rumor about Jenna and Craig. She told me first. She said she overheard them in the bathroom in the middle of the night. That's why all the other girls are gone. Those girls wanted to go to different homes anyway, closer to Austin. When the investigation started, they got their chance.

I just couldn't picture Jenna doing anything like that with Craig. He's a fat old man who barely even talks to us. And if Carrie really overheard them, why did she stay? She never explains anything she says. She says I think too much.

I was scared to leave. I didn't want to get new roommates, new foster parents. I had another panic attack when they asked me about it. So, Carrie and I stayed with Sandy's mom until the investigation was over. I guess Child Protective Services thought the same thing I did about Carrie's story, because it wasn't long until we were back at Sandy's house and the new girls started coming in.

When it was just the two of us, Carrie and I talked all the time, and I don't think I got on her nerves at all. I started to think we might be friends. We sort of were, even after the new girls came. None of them bothered me because Carrie had her ways of making them sorry if they made her mad.

I'm still not sure if being friends with Sandy was worth making Carrie mad at me. But I don't know what to do to fix it.

I wish I could switch rooms and have Caroline in my room. She's quiet and keeps to herself. I know the girls in her room tease her because of the birthmark on her face. But she's only nine, and I guess there are some restrictions about the age difference between kids that stay in the same room. Or maybe those are just Sandy's rules.

The last few words are squished up in the half-line at the bottom of the notebook paper. I can barely make them out.

The next page is a sketch on a thick piece of paper that barely fits into the binder. It's amazing. Beautiful. It's the face of a little girl with soft dark eyes and crooked bangs. There's a dark shadow swelling out of her right cheek and down below her jaw line. I know this is Caroline.

Never, in all of my memories of her, do I remember my mother drawing anything.

I hear heavy footsteps, and then I see the top of Colby's head as he comes around the camper. I slam the notebook closed and slide it under the cushion of the bench I'm sitting on. I don't want to share it with him yet. I'm not ready.

He opens the door, and I see him glance up at the bunk. Making sure Dad isn't here.

"First day of Christmas break," he says and slides into the bench across the table from me. "The twins are already gone."

"Is Shelby going to her dad's too?" I ask.

69

"Yeah, they just left for the bus station," Colby says and grins.

I know he'll miss the twins, but Aunt Rita is the only one who gets upset when Shelby goes away for the holidays.

"Shelby thinks her dad's going to get her the new iPhone for Christmas," Colby says. "Maybe I can get her old one if he does."

Shelby's dad is married and has a whole other set of kids and lives in Colorado. To Colby and me, Shelby's other family is like a set of mythical characters. Aunt Rita figures out how to get Shelby to the airport in Austin, and we don't see her for a couple of weeks. Then she comes home with all kinds of new crap, even more pissed off at the world than ever. She always says she should just go live with her dad and get away from all of us. But Colby and I both know that won't happen. We've both heard the fights between Aunt Rita and Shelby's dad over the phone.

"You might want to go get your balls out of her purse." That's Aunt Rita's favorite line for Shelby's dad. It's the stepmom who doesn't want Shelby around. Who can blame her?

Colby doesn't know who his dad is. Aunt Rita has never, not one time, talked to him about his dad. I think it's because she isn't smart enough to know how much it matters to him. Or she just doesn't care. Colby thinks there's more to the story. Like some mystery or scandal that Aunt Rita doesn't want to bring up. That's what makes him try so hard to be good. He knows there's someone out there. And he wants to make sure that one day that someone will really regret walking away.

But in the meantime, Colby and I are stuck here together. There isn't any other parent that's going to come and save us, not even for Christmas break.

"Hey," I say, looking for a reason to get out of the camper and away from my mother's binder. "Let's go to the library before all the teachers get off work and get the good books."

"We just got home," he says.

"What else is there to do?"

There really isn't anything better to do, so we walk slowly back to town, two weeks of nothing stretching out in front of us.

It's quiet on the square, only a few cars are in front of the courthouse. The Sherriff's truck is parked in the 15-minute spot in front of the dry cleaners. I can see him in there talking to the owner, his hip cocked up against the glass counter like he's John Wayne. The window of the flower shop is sprayed with fake snow, and just behind the glass is a twirling Christmas tree. The tea shop only serves lunch, and they are already closed for the day.

We come to the library thrift store before we get to the library itself, and I drag Colby inside. There's never anything actually good in there, but it's where I buy dishes and blankets and random things for the camper.

They have a Christmas display up too. It looks pitiful next to the flower shop. But there's a tabletop tree with decorations wired onto the branches.

"We need this," I tell Colby. "For the camper."

I expect him to roll his eyes and blow me off, but he doesn't. He bends one of the branches down and examines a foil-wrapped Styrofoam ornament.

"Where're you going to put it?" he asks. "It'll take up the whole table."

"So," I say, as if I'm determined to have it. But I'm not really sure I want it. I reach under the bottom row of branches and pull out the white paper tag where the price is written. An old lady wrote the numbers, I can tell. They're slanted and fancy. The tree costs fifteen dollars.

"I'll pay for half," Colby says. He always has more money than I do. He can go chop cedar for the Dawson's and make more in a weekend than I make in a month of babysitting.

The lady at the counter puts the tree back into its box for us, and I lug the thing with me into the library. Colby signs up for a computer to check his email, and I leave him there to go roam the shelves.

There's never anything new in the back. But the books in front, the new ones, are all vampire zombie end-of-the-world books. I'm tired of that already. I check out an old Stephen King book that I haven't read. I get Dune again, even though my name is the only one on the check-out card, and I practically have it memorized by now.

Then I wait for Colby. I sit in one of the uncomfortable chairs by the newspapers. I have to keep shifting around because the bones in my butt hurt from pressing into the hard seat.

We stay there until they close, and it's almost dark before we get back to the camper. I can see the glow of the TV through the kitchen window in Rita's house, but I know Colby doesn't want to go home. He doesn't want to be alone with his mother, and I can't blame him. I want Colby to go home so I can read more in my mother's journal. But when we pull the little

Christmas tree out of its box and plug it in, I'm glad I'm not alone. It's like magic how colored Christmas lights can make a drafty camper seem cozy.

By the time Colby gets up to go to his house, I'm trying hard not to fall asleep. He unplugs the Christmas tree before he goes. I don't turn on the light after he's gone, because he might see it and come back to check on me. I lay there in the dark and think about my mother. I'm trying to knit these two people together: the nervous girl who wrote those words and the ethereal mother of my memories.

Memories of my beautiful Momma, made right here in this camper, snuggled up in the bunk with her, giggling and playing "This Little Piggy." When I think of those times, when I block out the last part, I can still remember how special I felt. Charmed. Nothing could get me. Not Grandma, not Aunt Rita. I wasn't even scared of Uncle Ellis. I don't see how this girl in the journal managed that.

I'm not surprised when Dad doesn't come home. I wake up, and the sun is flooding the room, like the camper is lit up from inside. I only get up to pee and stretch before I reach under the cushion for Momma's notebook. Then I lie down and prop the book open on my knees, flipping past the first few pages I've already seen.

Ruby Bell   9/30/1994

Mrs. Patterson picked me as her office aide. I used to be assigned to the principal's office, running notes to classes for Mrs. Lynn. But now that I'm reassigned to Mrs. Patterson's office, there really isn't much to do.

She's the one who said I should start writing in a journal. I told her I didn't know what to write. She said I could start by writing about the day we first met, so that's what I wrote on my first day.

Then there were a bunch of schedule changes, and I had to run notes to classes and file a lot. I didn't have time to write for a few days. Now I don't know how to start again. So, she said I should write about my foster sisters.

That's weird, "foster sisters." Is that what it looks like to normal people? I'm an orphan. I don't have sisters.

Soooo... The little kids stay as far away from Carrie as possible. The only time Carrie ever pays attention to them is if she's staring them down when they get in her way.

Except, there's Genesis, the fourth grader who idolizes Carrie.

There's something about Genesis that seems too grown. She comes to the older kids with the weirdest stories. It's like little girl gossip about adult things. Things that happened at school, things the middle school girls are doing that they shouldn't. And she tells stories about her parents and their court dates and what their lawyers said and who told who off. The more shocking the story, the more she likes telling it. Like she's making an offering at an altar. She gets this crazy look in her eyes.

I always wonder how she got that way so young. Did she learn this from someone, or are some people just born to be vampires and feed on conflict and suffering?

Genesis is bossy, and she pushes the other younger girls around. It bothers me. She says stuff like "Oh my God, Caroline, I can't believe you ate all those pancakes.", or "Seriously, Becca, stop walking like that." Whenever I can, I try to get between them and tell her to mind her own business. It doesn't seem to bother Becca. But Caroline gets upset. I can see it in her face. And you'd think Genesis would stop when she sees Caroline's eyes fill up with tears, but she doesn't. She just gets meaner.

The middle school girls barely talk to each other, much less to us. Jenny's always quiet, with her head down. I try not to look directly at her, because I can just feel the fear coming off her in waves. I know exactly how she feels. She doesn't want anyone to see her. For her sake, I wish she had long thick hair, for better shelter. She looks so sad trying to hide behind her thin greasy strands.

Bobbi Jo needs a lot of help with schoolwork, but she's always happy. Mostly because she misses a lot of the undercutting that goes on. I guess it's not worth Carrie's time to try to slice Bobbi Jo up like she does me and Jenny, since Bobbi Jo doesn't get it anyway.

Marissa has thick dark hair and dark skin. Her blue eyes are a surprise when you get up close to her. Like jewels. I wish I could be like Marissa, even if she's only a seventh grader. She's tough and a little bit scary, which is good because Carrie doesn't mess with her either. Marissa doesn't talk much. But she's always watching with this disgusted look on her face, like she finds it all beneath her. I'd like to be able to rise above it all too. But I don't know how.

Mrs. Patterson bought me new shoes. Size eights. Keds. Real Keds. With the blue square on the back and everything. I saw the box beside her desk when I came in the first day, but I never thought for a second they could be mine.

As long as I've been a foster kid, I've gotten charity, either from secret shoppers at Christmas or donations from churches. It's usually worn-out pants, threadbare t-shirts, and stuffed animals. There's no end to the stuffed animals that people donate.

When we get new clothes, it's usually for Christmas and they're off-brand, wrong sized things from the discount store. Not that I'm ungrateful. Since I've been in foster care, Christmas never comes fast enough. I can remember being anxious for Christmas when my parents were still alive. But now being anxious means something else entirely.

Maybe someone like Carrie would see a Keds box and think about stealing those shoes. It always surprises me when she comes up with an idea like that. It's easier not to want things at all than go through that kind of trouble. You can't just wear a pair of Keds around our house and people not notice. I never wanted anything bad enough to get into that kind of trouble. Carrie acts like that makes me weird.

When Mrs. Patterson pulled that shoe box up onto her desk, I sort of wondered if they could be mine. But I kept my face blank. Or I tried to. She didn't make a big deal out of it when she gave them to me either. So, it was hard to know for sure. She just said, "You don't have any socks?"

It was so embarrassing. I always thought socks were to keep your ankles from getting cold. Or at school, the girls wear mix-matched socks, or more than one pair, stacked on top of each other. I like the way that looks. Tara is the girl that everyone copies when it comes to clothes.

I always wonder where she comes up with her ideas for outfits. The other day, she wore her Keds with two different colored pairs of socks and a denim mini skirt. And then she had matching tank tops stacked up the same as her socks. And suspenders. No one else would have ever worn suspenders to school. But everyone wants to now.

But I couldn't put my dirty feet into those perfectly white Keds. That's when I realized what socks are really for. And I really wished I had a pair. So, I had to wait.

Mrs. Patterson tried to get me to go ahead and wear them. But I didn't want to. I told her I'd wait until I had socks. I told her I had some at home. I did have socks. They weren't cool socks, but for the Keds, I could wear them.

I left the shoes in her office. I didn't want to carry them around school. That would have been even more embarrassing. People would take one look at that shiny shoe box, and the next thing they'd look at would be my feet. I really don't like anyone looking at me for too long. At all. Especially not at my feet.

So it wasn't until the next day, when I came back with my best pair of socks, that I actually put the Keds on.

I have Mrs. Patterson for second period so I got to wear them for most of the day. I went from worrying about my shoes falling apart, to worrying about getting them dirty. But they felt so much better on my feet.

Maybe I imagined people noticing my shoes. To me they were so white they practically glowed against my acid-wash jeans, which are yellow from all the washing. I know I've never been so aware of other people's shoes. I never really noticed just how many people have Keds. It seems like everyone has them but the kids that live with Sandy.

Carrie noticed them the second she sat beside me on the bus. I didn't expect her to be so mad. Her nostrils flared so wide her top lip turned up. She didn't even turn her head when she looked at me. She only rolled her eyes from my shoes up to my face. I swear I saw her ears go back. She said, "Were they handing new shoes out in the lunch line? Because I sure as hell didn't get any."

I didn't want to tell her Mrs. Patterson gave them to me. I had this vague fear that Carrie would try to get Mrs. Patterson in trouble. But I couldn't think fast enough to come up with a good lie. So I told her I got them from lost and found. I said no one claimed them for a year so that meant I could have them.

Carrie can't be an office aide because her grades aren't good enough. All her elective options are used up on the classes she takes trying to catch up on Math and Reading so she can pass the state test.

She didn't speak to me the rest of the way home. I tried to think of something to say, to get her talking again. I couldn't think of anything at all. I don't know why, but you can't just ask Carrie if she had a nice day.

She's just not like that. So, we rode in silence. It made the rest of the kids on the bus seem like a cloud of noisy craziness around us. I hate that feeling of dread, when I know she's mad and I just have to suffer.

The other kids from Sandy's got on the bus at the middle school, but they never sit with us. The elementary kids sit in the front of the bus. I could see the top of Caroline's head as she came up the steps, but then it disappeared behind the back of her big green seat.

All eight of us got off the bus at Sandy's house, and no one even noticed Carrie was mad. But when we got home, Carrie went straight to Sandy to complain about how I got new shoes, and she didn't.

In Sandy's house, every bedroom door opens up right into the big living room, which is sunk down, so we have to step up to go into our bedrooms. The only furniture in the living room is the mismatched sagging couches pushed against the two outside walls. The floors are all concrete, painted in this green color that reminds me of a tennis-court. Sandy says it's easier to keep clean than carpet. The big room feels like an empty cave.

Sandy came out of the toddler room when she heard Carrie yelling. She looked at my feet. She couldn't help but notice my shoes, even without Carrie's tantrum. My Keds were still bright white because I walked slow down the drive and made sure not to let my feet kick each other.

"I cleaned out the lost and found," I answer before she can ask. "They'd been in there for over a year."

"A brand-new pair of shoes?" Sandy says. "Who loses a brand-new pair of shoes?"

I'm lying. And it feels horrible. And the way Sandy is looking at me, I start to wonder if I actually might have stolen these shoes. Carrie was giving me this horrible look. So, I told Sandy that Mrs. Patterson said I could keep them, trying to work my way back to the truth.

And then Sandy changes. Like a curtain goes up behind her eyes or something. She turns to Carrie and tells her if she kept her grades up, she could have been the one cleaning out the lost and found. I should have been relieved, but I wasn't.

Carrie quit looking at me. She turned on Sandy and started yelling at her. She said things like, "Are you fucking kidding me?" and "How is that fair? If she gets shoes, we should all get shoes."

And Sandy was all "Carrie, I'm not going to argue with you. I can't afford to buy new shoes for everyone." And Carrie said she should call that school and tell them not to give shoes to little suck-asses so they can prance around in them for everyone else to have to watch.

Sandy looked at me, and I knew she was mad at me for starting trouble, but she didn't yell at me. She turned into "professional foster mom" and said, "Now Carrie, I understand why you're upset, But I can't allow that kind of language."

Carrie walked off while Sandy was still talking. She went to our room and slammed the door. I saw Genesis, leaning on the frame of her own bedroom door. She looked mad with her hip cocked out, her belly poking out from between her jeans and t-shirt. I saw Caroline behind her, looking at my shoes.

Just about everything I've ever owned was in that room with Carrie, and there's no telling what Carrie will do when she's mad. But I didn't dare go in there.

Sandy glared at me and then went back over the baby gate into the toddler room. I stood there like an idiot for a second with nowhere to go. Then Sandy called me in there to empty a potty chair.

I am so pissed when I read the next part, I want to go back in time and find Carrie and beat the living shit out of her. I want to go back in time and inhabit my mother's life and take charge of it. I can't stand this. There's no fixing it now. But I know exactly what I'd do if I could.

Mrs. Patterson looked mad when she saw me wearing my old shoes to school the next day. She didn't yell at me or anything. But her eyes got big, and she kept looking at my feet and back at my face, like she just couldn't believe what she was seeing. She was saying, "You gave them to Carrie?" and "Do they even fit Carrie?"

They didn't fit Carrie. They were too big. Carrie is short. Or maybe she just has short arms and tiny hands and feet. She just seems big because she's sort of round, and because she's so loud. But I lied and said they fit Carrie.

I don't know why, but I felt like I might be losing something big with Mrs. Patterson. Bigger than the shoes. But what choice did I have?

Anyway, it wasn't like I could explain. She didn't say anything to me for the rest of my class period. So, when I got back from running notes, I wrote it all down in my journal. I guess this is why people have journals.

CHAPTER 8

Marissa plays volleyball at the middle school. She's the only one of us even remotely athletic. And now that she started playing games, Sandy says we can stay in town to watch them if we want.

Carrie's over being mad at me since I gave her the shoes. She's over everything, even about being Sandy's favorite. And now that we're back to being friends, she wants me to stay with her for Marissa's games.

Except Carrie doesn't watch the games. I found that out at the first game, when we walked into the gym and up into the bleachers where two of her friends were waiting for her. Her friends have piercings and tattoos on their fingers, and they wear leather gloves with the fingers cut off. And most of them don't even go to school anymore, so we don't stay in the gym for long.

We meet up with Carrie's other friends at the park. Not the new park by the fire station with the red and yellow monkey bars. The old park, down Mission Hill Road. The splintered seesaw is overgrown with weeds, and the swing set is only a rusty frame. There's a path worn through the overgrown grass to the wooden picnic table where kids like us hang out.

They don't like me, but she drags me along. They ignore me for the most part, aside from occasionally offering me a drag on whatever they're smoking. And I sit there, or stand, if there isn't room at the table. I never have anything to say. I hardly ever know what they're talking about. And I get the feeling I don't want to know.

They use names for drugs I've never heard of and talk about people they buy drugs from. They talk about who burned who for how much money, or how much coke. Who OD'd on cheese. Whose mom is in jail. Who's living under the bridge because he can't stand his parents.

Most of these kids would be in a place like Sandy's, but they have just enough of a family left that the state can't force them into a stranger's house. And some of them aren't kids anymore. Rita's brother Jimmy is twenty. He isn't always around. They say he runs with the Hoyle family. I don't know who the Hoyle family is, but Carrie's friends act like they're celebrities. Dangerous celebrities.

There's a tall boy, named Eric, who dropped out because the school doesn't allow hair dyed an "unnatural color." Carrie's friends like him because he talks so much. I think it covers the silence of the others. But I also think his talking is going to get him in trouble one day.

Like the time he was just trying to make small talk with Jimmy. He said something like, "I saw you riding with Ellis Hoyle the other day," or whatever. And Jimmy said, "So?" and "What are you the town crier?" And Eric didn't get the hint. I really wished he would be quiet. But then he started asking Jimmy about some rumors he heard about Ellis. I didn't get it exactly. He said, "I heard Ellis shot some guy up with Drano for trying to talk to his connection."

Jimmy was sitting at the picnic table smoking a cigarette. He didn't answer right away. He flicked his cigarette and squinted at Eric, like he couldn't believe anyone could be so stupid. Then he said, "I don't know where you people hear this shit. That is some urban legend bullshit if I ever heard it."

And it was tense for a minute, then Carrie laughed first. Then everyone else laughed. Sort of. Until Jimmy pointed at Eric with the hand holding his cigarette and said, "And if you're smart, you'll keep your fucking fairytales to yourself."

I have just read my mother's version of how she met my father. And all I can tell is that she thought Dad was dangerous. She described Uncle Ellis as a stranger. My mother, still completely innocent of this life, the life where she left me. Am I about to read the moment where her life turned? How I ended up here? Do I want to? I still can't see how I came from these two people.

There's a page of doodles between this sheet of notebook paper and the next. On it is a sketch of a hand holding a cigarette between the first two fingers. The other fingers are folded back. There's a tattoo in the soft place between the thumb and index finger. Two crooked Js. I can just imagine it pointing at some boy named Eric. There's also a sketch of some Keds. Not whole shoes, just a view of them from the back, side-by-side. The letters on the logos are drawn with the tiniest touch of perspective. They look like they're coming off the page.

There are other random sketches on the page. I know what some of them must be, like the baby-gate floating by itself in white space. And there are things I don't understand, like the teddy bear in a rocking chair. On the back side, the whole page is taken up with a picture of a tennis-court, net and all, with couches along two sides, and plain wooden doors along the other two. This makes me smile. It's a relief to know there was more to my mother than she could put into words.

I've had enough. I close the journal and look around the camper. The Christmas tree is taking up the entire table, just like Colby said it would. I feel like I just got back from outer space. The whole place looks different now.

I've always known my mother was fifteen when she had me. One year older than I am now. But that was just a number. A statistic. A circumstance.

Now I can hear her voice in my head. I can imagine a girl like her in the halls at school. An outsider, like me. I imagine this camper through her eyes. I picture myself coming here, living with someone like Dad and his family. I don't think I could face it. But she tried to be happy. She must have had some hope, to hang on as long as she did.

I'm exhausted after reading this. I don't know how I'll deal with what I might find in her words. But I have to know. Anyway, she said I was strong. That's how I know I can face it. I'm just scared.

Rita Jennings is pregnant again. And that isn't really anything to write about. There are two other pregnant girls at school. One of them was even a cheerleader. But Carrie told me it's Rita's second baby. And her first kid is by her old math teacher. Mr. Dempsey.

And I wouldn't normally believe rumors like that, because people have been saying that Tara was sleeping with the basketball coach, and that this other girl, Madison, went down on Mrs. Trujillo in the girls' bathroom. And on and on it goes. People just make up stuff.

But I was in Mrs. Patterson's office when I overheard a teacher in the hallway talking about it. The teacher was talking about "that girl," and she said it was no surprise she was pregnant again because "that girl wouldn't rest until she ruined that poor man's career." And she said she couldn't count the times she'd go to Mr. Dempsey's classroom after school, and Rita was there, "as if she ever cared about her math grade."

I heard Mrs. Patterson say, "Rita is a product of her environment, and a child. He was a grown man. He had the responsibility."

Then the voice told Mrs. Patterson she was naïve for wanting to save the world. And "that's only going to break your heart, or worse." But then this voice started talking about "those kinds of people." She said they don't know what it means to be a child. She said that "those kinds of people are hell bent on destruction from the time they know how to use their bodies to get what they want."

She called Mrs. Patterson Sarah. I didn't picture her as a Sarah.

Mrs. Patterson sounded kind of sad when she told the voice that it wasn't an appropriate conversation for the hallway. I felt sorry for Mrs. Patterson. And I felt even worse for giving Carrie my shoes. She was trying to help me, and I'm sure she thought I was just ungrateful. Just another one of "those kinds of people."

I read and re-read the first part of this short little section. Colby's dad was a math teacher. Might still be a math teacher. Mr. Dempsey. The answer to the unspeakable question is sitting, unapologetically, in front of me on the page.

No drum roll. No curtain slowly pulled back. Nothing to warn me that it's coming. She just states it as a commonly known fact.

How commonly known? My mother calls it a rumor.

Did the kids of that time grow up and whisper about it in front of their own kids? Of course they did. They all whisper in front of their kids. About everybody. Especially us.

They all have to know.

Am I supposed to tell Colby?

I turn on my side and pull my blanket over my head. I stay there until my stomach starts growling, and then I get up and make myself a bowl of cereal.

I know I'm not going to tell him, and I feel guilty about it. He has a right to know. I don't have the right to keep this from him, any more than his mother does. But telling him about his dad would mean telling him about my mother's journal.

I don't know how to talk about my mother. To anyone. So much about her is still locked in that voiceless place in my mind, the murky part that swallowed me when I was six. And I don't want anyone talking to me about her. I love Colby, but not even him. After everything that happened, no one has that right.

By the time I get through eating I think I'm ready to look Colby in the face without giving myself away. I don't change out of my flannel pajama bottoms and t-shirt. I just slip my feet into my tennis shoes, put on my hoody and open the camper door.

It's chilly, but the sun is bright. It's too much for my eyes, for my mood. He's already outside, banging around under the hood of his mom's car.

"You slept late," he says. "You sick or something?"

"Dude, it's Saturday," I answer. "You're supposed to sleep late."

There's trash burning in the rusted out fifty-five-gallon barrel. He's been outside for a while.

"Can you try to start it?"

I leave the primered door of the Grand Am open and sit behind the wheel. There's dinging when I turn the ignition, and I can hear something come on in front of the dash. But the car doesn't even try to start.

"Okay stop," he says. Then a few minutes later, "Okay, again."

Still the dinging and humming, but nothing else.

Colby comes around to the driver's side. He's looking at me, but he's thinking about the problem.

"I guess I could try the ignition." He rubs the grease off his wrench with a dirty red rag. "I think ignition switches are cheap. Want to go see if they have one at O' Reilly's?"

I shrug. "I guess it's something to do."

"If I get this car running again, maybe mom will let me drive us to school."

I don't see that happening. Every time he fixes her car, she only lets him use it to go to the store for her, or the Laundromat. But there's no point in saying that. I'm not going to be the one to squash his hope.

As we walk into town with the sun shining in our eyes, I think about Mr. Dempsey. I wish I knew what he looked like. I keep sneaking looks at Colby. I've only ever seen Aunt Rita in Colby's face. And everything that isn't Aunt Rita is just Colby. But now I look at his eyes, thankfully nothing like Aunt Rita's and Dad's, and I realize they must be Dempsey eyes.

I can't think of Colby's dad as a pervert. Maybe I hate Aunt Rita so much I automatically imagine Mr. Dempsey as her victim. Like she raped a grown man when she was fifteen and then kept father and son apart for spite. I know it isn't possible. But all this good in Colby had to come from somewhere, didn't it? It didn't come from the Jennings' side, that's for sure. And I love Colby so much, I can't help but be sad for the dad who never got to see how awesome he is.

As we walk up to the parts store, I see Sheila drive by in her Toyota Four Runner. She must be out Christmas shopping or something. She doesn't notice us, but I see a glimpse of Jathan in the back seat. The brake lights come on, then the blinker, and the car turns into the Dairy Queen down the street.

Colby talks to the man behind the counter *forever* about whether the starter has gone bad again, or if the ignition switch was the problem the whole time. And they look over part numbers and diagrams until I think I'm going to scream. Because what I really want to do is talk Colby into going to Dairy Queen.

The switch is almost forty dollars, way more than he thought it would be, but he puts the money on the counter. The O'Reilly guy must have noticed the nervous look on Colby's face because he says again that Colby can bring it back if he needs to.

Thankfully, the Four Runner is still parked at the Dairy Queen when we come out.

"Want to get an ice cream cone?" I ask.

"I want to know if this is going to work," he answers and holds up the O' Reilly bag. "That was my last forty dollars."

"I have some money. A cone is only like a dollar or something."

He huffs a little, but gives in.

When we get inside the Dairy Queen, I search the dining room. Jathan's face lights up when he sees me.

"Hey there bud!" I call out to him, and Sheila turns around.

I try to get Colby to go with me, but he won't, so I leave him by the door. I know it's because he's nervous to be around someone like Sheila. Or Mrs. Miller. That's what he calls her.

I go over and slide onto the bench beside Jathan. I just plan on saying hi and talking for a second. I rub his head a little and then kiss his forehead.

"I missed you after school yesterday," I tell him. And the truth is, I feel like I've gone a million years and even more miles since I saw him last. "Did you have a blast at your Christmas party?"

"Yeah, we had sooo many snacks," he said, "And Emilio stuck Sour Punch Straws up his nose. You should have seen it."

"Oh my gosh! Didn't that burn?" I ask.

"You didn't tell me that," Sheila says.

"I forgot," he tells her, then turns to me. "Yeah, it did burn!" He's so into what he's telling me, he's nodding and gesturing and making faces. He isn't a small kid, but sometimes, like right now his hands look too big for his skinny arms. It makes me laugh. "He started sneezing and crying, and he had to go to the nurse. It was so FUNNY!"

"That sounds terrible," Sheila says.

"Emilio is always doing stuff like that. He can shoot milk out of his eyes. It's so awesome."

"I better not hear about you trying any of that." Sheila's trying to be all stern and serious, but he's so cute, she finally smiles too.

"Dude, nobody's that crazy," he says. "Except Emilio."

Colby's standing by the door looking at me. He's irritated that I left him there, and I don't blame him. He doesn't have any money, so he's just stuck. I know I have to go, but I don't want to.

Then Sheila puts her empty wrappers back on their tray, and I realize they're finished eating, so I get up. Jathan slides out of the booth after me. I'm tempted to kiss the top of his head again before he goes, because I don't know when I'll see him again. But Sheila's looking all formal with her keys in her hand, so I just ruffle his red cowlick and nudge him with my elbow.

After they leave, I order two small cones from the girl behind the counter. While she's making them, I turn around because I want to apologize to Colby. That's when I notice Mrs. Patterson. She's sitting with another woman in a booth toward the back of the room. She's watching me. I guess she's been watching me the whole time.

I'm frozen, gazing at her, lost for a minute. It was only yesterday she handed me that notebook. A million miles and years ago. I haven't seen everything in it. I know she has.

I don't want to share this with her. With anyone.

"Excuse me," the counter girl says, making me jump. I turn around to see her holding the ice cream cones.

Colby reaches past me to take his. "Can we go home now?" He's still irritated.

"Yeah," I say, and take my cone.

I try to smile at Mrs. Patterson on the way out. It's almost painful. I'm sure it looks as bad as it feels. I'm not sure why I smile, except maybe because she saw me with Jathan. And because I want her to know I'm fine. I don't need to talk to anyone.

The ignition switch fixes Aunt Rita's car. She even comes out onto her steps when she hears it start.

"That's great," she says, standing there holding her Virginia Slim. "It'd been better if you'd figured this out the other day. Then I wouldn't have put Shelby on a Greyhound."

Colby doesn't answer. He just turns the car off, gets out and closes the hood.

I'm sitting on the pull-down step of the camper, watching Aunt Rita. She's built like a barrel with spindly, veiny legs sticking out of her shorts. She has enormous hair. I can't imagine what it would look like if she just left it alone. She never actually goes anywhere, but she still spends the first part of her day in rollers and the second part with a shellacked dust bunny on her head. Her face is hard. Her eyes and mouth are all shrunk down with hate, just like Dad's.

I can't imagine anyone who could take advantage of her. And I cannot imagine the man who could be seduced by her.

"You got money for gas now?" Aunt Rita asks, like she's saying, "Alright smarty pants." Not grateful at all.

But I see Grandma looking out her window. Of course, she heard the car start. She's probably been watching us the whole time. She taps on the glass to get Colby's attention and then motions for him to come over. I bet Colby's going to get gas money from her if he'll run her errands. But I'm not about to go over there with him to find out what she wants. I toss him the peace sign and get up to go inside.

A few minutes later, Colby's at my door. Grandma wants him to go to the meat market in Fairview to get those giant packages of hamburger meat and sacks of flour they sell. She divides up the meat and freezes it in packages that she uses for her Hamburger Helper or spaghetti or whatever. You'd think Grandma was some kind of invalid frontier woman or something the way she likes to stock food and save flour sacks.

He's asking me to go with him to the meat market. And I really really don't want to. I think staying might be my best chance to read more of my mother's journal, but I feel sorry for him. Aunt Rita has already taken most of the fun out of getting the car fixed. I say yes, and put on my shoes.

I take a second to look down at my shoes, and I'm grateful. I feel rich, really. My shoes fit. Things could be a lot worse.

It's about fourteen miles to Fairview. We probably should have made the first trip in the car a shorter one. It would've been better to find out the battery wasn't charging in Oak Grove. And it might not be so bad if we didn't have thirty pounds of hamburger meat and a twenty-pound sack of flour to deal with.

Colby has his cell phone, but there isn't anyone to call. Except Dad.

And that makes me think hard about taking the food back into the store for a refund and just walking home. Dad hasn't been home in a couple of days. There's no telling why. On a binge. On a run. Either way, not of any use.

But the car has to get home somehow. Colby has the hood up. He's saying something about the alternator or battery connection. And he looks like he's about to cry.

I take his phone and dial Dad's number. And I'm not really surprised when Uncle Ellis answers.

I clear my throat when I hear his voice. "It's Jade." My voice cracks anyway.

"Your dad's asleep," he says. "What's up?"

"Our car broke down in Fairview," I tell him. "Can you wake him up?"

"Nah," Uncle Ellis laughs. "He ain't gonna wake up. What's wrong with yer car? Who you with?"

"Colby thinks the battery cable was loose, and it didn't charge or something. We just need a jump," I say. "Or maybe the battery's bad."

"Where in Fairview?" he asks.

"We're at Lawson's Meat Market."

I know he's going to come for us. Dad must have crashed. Uncle Ellis doesn't ever have that problem. He's practically one of those straight-edge people. He just smokes a little weed every now and then. But even when he's high, he's way too intense.

He only takes twenty minutes to get to us. And he barely talks when he gets out of his truck. He drives a big red Ford with a cow-pusher on the front. I guess that big bumper is intimidating, just like Uncle Ellis, but he doesn't have it for looks. The Hoyle family has a lot of land, a ranch actually, with a herd of cows and everything. I guess all that land comes in handy.

"Pop the hood," he tells Colby and then flips open the toolbox in the bed of his truck. He takes out his jumper cables and a crescent wrench, moving like a cat or some predatory animal. He's wearing Levi's and a plain red t-shirt that isn't too small but doesn't hide his massive chest and arms. A tribal tattoo comes up his neck and covers most of the right side of his buzzed head.

He catches me watching him, locks eyes on me and cocks his head.

I blink fast and drop my eyes.

He goes back to the car, talking to Colby like they hang out all the time, or something. Aunt Rita threatened Colby with his life if she ever heard of him talking to the Hoyles. Honestly, that might be the only time I've ever thought Aunt Rita was smart.

"You got this car runnin' all by yerself?"

"Yes, Sir." Colby is scared of Uncle Ellis, just like everyone else. "It was the ignition switch."

"Then how'd you fuck up the battery?"

Colby's eyes get big.

"I'm just kidding," Uncle Ellis says and shoves Colby. It's supposed to be friendly but it's not. "I think it's cool as shit. I didn't think kids your age worked on cars anymore."

Colby stands back while Uncle Ellis leans forward and does something with the battery cables. Then they hook up the jumper cables, and I'm pretty sure I only start breathing again when I hear the car start.

I'm walking between the car and Uncle Ellis' truck when I feel his monstrous hand on my shoulder. It stops me, holds me right where I stand. It's like someone poured ice water down my back.

"You're lucky you look just like yer momma, you know that?" he says into my ear from behind.

I can't even swallow, much less talk.

"You need anything?" he asks. "I promised her I'd take care of you."

"You promised Dad you'd take care of *her*," I whisper.

His hand squeezes my shoulder and pulls me backward, just a little. "What's that?" he says. I feel the bones in my shoulder straining in his grip.

"I'm good," I manage to say, louder. "Dad's got it."

"Yer Dad's sprawled out on my living room floor. He thought he was seeing little green men a few hours ago," He laughs, and I feel my hair move. "You need something, you call me."

"Yes, Sir," I say, and he lets me go.

I get in the car, and Colby is so relieved. He's smiling and scanning stations on the radio. He has gas money, and the car is running. He calls one of his friends from school and makes a plan to hang out. I'm grateful it doesn't involve me.

When we get home, I tell him I'm going home to take a shower. I'm not helping him take the groceries to Grandma's. I've put up with enough for one day.

I hear Rita's voice outside, asking "Where the hell have you been?"

After my shower, I flop down on my bench, back in my PJs even though it's only four o' clock. When I hear Colby driving off, I pull my mother's notebook out from under the cushion. I guess I don't have to worry about Dad coming home.

CHAPTER 9

Mrs. Patterson wants me to write about my parents. She thinks it'll help with my panic attacks. I don't see how it could. I barely remember my parents. It wasn't that long ago, but I guess I have amnesia or something, because I honestly don't even remember what my dad looked like. I kind of remember my mom. She had dark straight hair, not red and curly like mine. But it was frosted. I remember that I saw her with foil in her hair once or twice. Maybe we went to the salon together.

The only real thing I have left of my mother is the ruby necklace she gave me. I can't wear it. Carrie would probably steal it if she knew I had it. I started keeping it in my journal so I could at least see it all the time.

I don't know exactly what happened to my parents. There was an accident. I sort of remember the hospital. I think my grandparents came to see me there. My dad's parents. But I might just be making that memory up because that's what the social workers said. That they came to see me. So maybe I just made up a memory to go with the story.

Anyway, I don't know why all of this matters now. They didn't want me. I think they were very old when they had my dad, so they were too old to raise their grandkid. In my memory, they were kind of stiff people. Not the kind to hug or anything. My dad was like that too, I think. Maybe that's why I can't remember him. I think he worked all the time, or he was busy with something. It didn't bother me though. He just wasn't that important to me, I guess.

But my mother hugged. She sang and laughed, and I remember dancing around the living room with her. I even remember jumping on the bed with my mom. That seems insane to me now. I can't imagine any mother doing that, so it makes me wonder if I made that memory up too.

We lived up by Dallas. I had my own room. My own bathroom too. We had a big house with a big yard. I do remember that. There was a playhouse in the back. It was a real playhouse, not like those plastic ones, but it was wood and had shingles and lights and wallpaper.

The truth is, I know my daddy was rich, and his family was rich. And rich people are not nice. They don't like to be bothered.

But that's all I remember.

I don't like riding in cars now. The van doesn't bother me, and the bus is fine. But cars give me panic attacks. Writing can't fix that. Not riding in cars is the only thing that helps.

So, Mrs. Patterson wants to know where my mother's parents are. Like she's trying to find a home for me. I hate that. I don't want her to call people and ask them if they'll take me in. I'm embarrassed for them to be put on the spot. I don't know what would be worse, them saying they don't want me, or them being guilted into taking me.

So, I tell her I don't know.

And I really don't know. My mom didn't speak to her parents. I think her parents were divorced or something. And they never even knew about me. So why would I want to find them?

I'm only writing all of this for Mrs. Patterson. She isn't mad about the shoes anymore, and that's a huge relief. But I don't think she's going to buy me anything else. I don't blame her. I don't want anything anyway. It's too much trouble.

She keeps saying that I'm smart. That I have so much potential. I think she's making that up. There are kids at school in every club and on every team. They take dance classes and music lessons, and they do community service for National Honor Society. They have potential.

I don't do anything, and I don't want to do anything. I don't want to be scared anymore.

I just want to fade away.

There it is. My mother trying to slip away. It was there all along.

I guess I can't blame Dad and Uncle Ellis and Aunt Rita and Grandma entirely. I still hate them. But Momma just wasn't made for this life. She should have been able to stay in her playhouse world, with a mom who took her to the salon and jumped on the bed with her.

If there was a way to go back and fix it, I'd give up my existence so she could stay there.

<u>Ruby Bell</u><u>12/2/1994</u>

Since Rita Jennings got pregnant, she quit smoking. She quit everything. Now I'm not the only one standing there like an idiot at the park when everyone else leaves to go do whatever they do. She stays with me.

Since she got pregnant, she gets food stamps and sells them to some lady she knows for half the cash. So, she has money, and sometimes instead of going to the park, we go through K-Mart and look at baby stuff.

Sandy won't let me go to Rita's house. She says the whole Jennings family is trouble. Like the girls that live with Sandy aren't? I don't think Rita is half as bad as Carrie.

I think Sandy's worried that I'm going to talk to Mrs. Patterson about her. I think that's why she's been so much nicer to me since Mrs. Patterson brought me home that day. After she made me clean potty chairs, she seemed kind of nervous around me for a while. She started saying things, like "Now don't go running back to Mrs. Patterson and tell her I'm being mean to you," when it's my turn to do dishes. And then she smiles like she's joking.

She should know there isn't anything to worry about with me. I don't want to have to move. I want to tell her that, but I'm afraid it would just make things even more weird.

Ruby Bell   1/13/1995

I missed the bus again the other day. And this time I got a ride from Rita's brother Jimmy. I was about to freak out. Rita told me to calm down already, that we'd figure something out. So, Jimmy has a truck, and Rita asked him if he could take me home. And he said he didn't mind. Like it was no big deal at all.

I rode between him and Rita, and I wasn't even nervous around him. To me, that is a really big deal. I mean, he didn't really talk to me, so I didn't have any reason to freak out. And I guess I was more worried about getting in trouble with Sandy than sitting beside him in the truck.

He pulled his truck right up behind the bus, and I got out and walked to the house with the rest of the kids, like nothing ever happened.

Carrie saw his truck, but she just laughed like it was funny. And it was not a big deal at all. I was kind of proud of myself. I didn't have a meltdown, and I didn't get in trouble. I thought it was fine.

But then later that night, it was my turn to carry out the trash, and Craig was by the dumpster. It was almost dark, and he scared me half to death. He said, "I saw you in that truck with Jimmy Jennings."

I guess I've never really looked at Craig before. I never noticed his freckles. I always thought he was blondish, but he really has dark hair.

And for a second I got this weird idea that he wants to be invisible. But not because he's scared, like me and Jenny. I'm sure that's just me being crazy again.

He laughed at me and told me not to worry. He said he wasn't going to tell Sandy. Then he took the trash bags out of my hands and swung them into the dumpster. I thought it was weird that he was telling me he wouldn't tell his wife. I thought maybe he was just like the rest of us, scared of Sandy.

But then he asked me, "Are you having sex with him?" Flat out, just like that. And I didn't even know how to answer. The way he asked the question scared me, out there away from the house, with the light fading.

I told him I don't even know Jimmy, that he's just Rita's brother. And then he said, "She's the one that was banging that teacher, right?" I just stared at him. It was like he caught me in some kind of trap. I could feel the panic coming. I knew it was going to take over. Then I was just as afraid of the panic as I was of Craig. I knew he would tell Sandy on me. Maybe tell her things that aren't even true.

Because he said, "So you and your friend Rita are into older men then?" And I said, "No." But then he smiled, and it creeped me out. So I wanted to be clear and I said, "I'm not into anyone." But he just kept smiling, and then he looked down. He was talking to my chest when he said that was good, that I'm too young to get into trouble like Rita did.

I guess I was waiting for him to leave me, to go back to the house first. But he just kept standing there, then he said, "Come on," and made me go in front of him. Then he held the screen door open for me, so I had to stand right by him while I opened the other door. While I was trying to get it open, he said, "Don't worry. Your secrets are safe with me."

I wanted to tell him I don't have any secrets, but mostly I just wanted away from him.

Ruby Bell   2/4/1995

I haven't written in a while because I'm so mad. So, I guess Mrs. Patterson has reported Sandy for things. That's what Carrie said. Something about Mrs. Patterson turning Sandy in for not spending money on the kids like she was supposed to or something.

It all started because Mrs. Patterson found this old notebook, a Trapper Keeper. And she said I could have it to keep my stuff in. And Carrie was making fun of me. She said the rainbows and hearts were stupid. And then she told me the only reason Mrs. Patterson is so nice to me is because she's trying to get Sandy in trouble again. Like they have some kind of battle going on.

And then she made fun of me for looking sad. She said, "You didn't think she really liked you?" And she laughed and said, "You did! You thought you were something special, didn't you?"

I told her I didn't. I told her no one's that stupid. But then I had to look out the window until I wasn't worried about crying any more.

I guess I'm Mrs. Patterson's spy. No wonder she's so interested in me. So much for having someone to talk to. Now, when I really need someone, all I have is this stupid journal. I get so sick of people. Everyone just uses each other.

I don't know how I barely noticed Craig before, because now it seems like he's always around. I kept telling myself I was being crazy. He's always been around. I just never paid attention because the house is so full of so many people.

Then I went into the kitchen to get a glass of water a couple of nights ago, and he was in there. He told me I could have a Coke, but I knew Sandy would have a fit if I drank one of her Cokes. No one is allowed to drink her Cokes. But he pulled it out of the fridge, popped the can open, and handed it to me. I told him I didn't want it, but he made me take a drink of it.

Then he took it out of my hand and sat it on the counter behind me. But he didn't move back after he set it down, so he had me pinned. I almost knocked the Coke over trying to hold myself up, trying to keep my back from breaking on the edge of the counter. The top of my head was grinding into the cabinet above me. But I didn't make a noise. I don't know why I didn't make any noise. I just knew I'd be the one in trouble if Sandy came in. And God help me if Carrie saw him on me, it would ruin everything all over again.

And then he said, "Maybe you can show me a little of what you gave that Jennings boy." I was wearing my long night gown, so his hand didn't get very far between my legs, but he tried. Then he tried to reach between my legs from the back, and then he gave up on that and started pinching me on the chest, hard.

I still didn't make any noise. I was holding my breath. I don't know what made him stop. I think he heard a noise or something, but I don't know how he could have, he was breathing so hard. He got real still and turned his head like he was listening. Then he backed away from me and told me to drink my Coke. I was shaking so bad, I almost dropped the can, but I did what he said. I picked it up and took a long drink. Then he said he knew I liked older men, and he knew I came into the kitchen looking for him. I tried to tell him no. I shook my head, but I didn't look at him. I told him I was just thirsty and asked him if I could please just go to bed.

And then he got mad and said, "Yeah, you better get in bed. You wouldn't want Sandy to find out you've been sneaking around at night. Drinking her Cokes. She'll probably ship you off when she finds out about you and Jimmy."

I started to cry, and I told him I didn't even know Jimmy Jennings. And then he laughed, but not in a nice way. He said not to worry, he wasn't going to rat me out. And then he told me to go to bed, like it was his idea.

Ruby Bell   2/6/1995

I skipped school today. I got off the bus and walked to the park like I was walking through a fog. Then I sat at the picnic table by myself all morning, not really thinking anything, just glad to be away from school.

I don't know why Jimmy Jennings came by the park that morning. It's not like the park is in town where people are always driving by. It's practically buried out in the weeds. The only thing down Mission Hill Road is a junk yard. Maybe he was going there. I didn't ask.

He stopped when he saw me there and rolled down his window. He asked me why I wasn't in school. I shrugged and put my head down on the table, trying to hide inside my folded arms.

He sat there for a while, his truck idling. Then I heard sticks breaking under his tires. I lifted my head and saw him parking his truck in the grass then getting out of his truck. I guess my face was all splotchy like it gets when I cry, because he kind of looked worried when he got closer.

He asked me if I was okay as he slid onto the bench across from me. He was so careful, like he was afraid he would hurt me by shaking the table. I told him I was okay, but then I started crying all over again. I tried to cover my face, but he pulled my hands away and pulled my chin up.

He told me, "It's okay. I promise. Whatever it is, it's gonna be okay."

But I shook my head and tried to tell him it wasn't going to be okay. And then he asked if someone had hurt me, but I didn't answer him.

And then he said, "Come on, Ruby, you have to tell me what happened, or I won't be able to help."

I guess it surprised me that he knew my name. It was enough to help me stop bawling. I wiped my nose on my sleeve. I told him I was fine and there wasn't anything anyone could do. And he laughed. That surprised me again.

He said, "Try me. You'd be amazed what I can do."

His smile was just like the Cheshire cat from that Disney movie. All teeth and up to no good. I kind of laughed too.

Then he said, "There, now that's what I'm talking about." He asked me who needed to pay for making me cry. He said he would take care of it.

I laughed again. Because at first, I thought he was joking. But he took my hand, the one with the snot on the sleeve, and pulled it toward him. He looked me hard in the face and said he really wanted to know. He wasn't smiling.

So I told him.

Ruby Bell   2/13/1995

Craig said he caught his ear on something at work. But he was pretty vague about how exactly. He just came home one night and one of his earlobes was gone.

Sandy made him go to the doctor to see if he needed stitches, but they just put a bandage over it and sent him back to work. She keeps nagging him about workman's comp, but he won't fill out the form.

He hasn't looked my way since. In fact, he leaves the room when I come in.

Ruby Bell   2/15/1995

I asked Jimmy if he did it. It wasn't like we planned to meet. I just snuck over to the park after second period. I think as long as I at least go to Mrs. Patterson's, I'm less likely to get caught. She's the only one keeping up with me.

Jimmy said he had no idea what I was talking about, but he was grinning, a half-moon of a smile. And I said, "You did! You did!" I punched him on the arm and told him, "Oh my gosh! I cannot believe you did that!"

He said he didn't do anything, and he didn't know what I was talking about. He caught my hand and held it when I tried to land a second punch. He said sometimes bad things just happen to bad people.

I couldn't help myself. I was grinning back at him. He said that making me smile was like winning a prize. I got embarrassed and tried to stop smiling. Then my face just got hot, and I smiled even more. I put my other hand up to cover my mouth. He pulled that one down and held it too. He told me to look at him. He told me not to ever be afraid to smile, ever, in front of anyone.

I stopped smiling then. All of a sudden, I felt like crying.

I thought he might try to kiss me or something. I mean I didn't know what to expect. No one ever talked to me like that. I never felt so safe around anyone before. But he didn't kiss me. Not exactly. He just pressed the backs of my fingers against his mouth for a second. I took a step toward him, maybe kind of hoping he would kiss me.

Then I felt stupid for that because he let my hands go and told me to go back to school.

Leaving him was like walking away from a fire or something. I felt the cold creeping back in with every step.

I know I should be scared of him. So many people are scared of him. But I'm just not. In those few minutes I spent with him, I was not afraid of anything.

CHAPTER 10

The sun is down now. I plug in my Christmas tree. It's Saturday night, and that's about all I know for sure. Everything else is questionable. Especially these people I've lived with my whole life. My family. Aunt Rita and my Momma were friends. Dad was my Momma's hero.

I'm struggling. And it's not just that I want to come out of my skin at the thought of Dad kissing the back of Momma's hands and talking so smooth. I just can't believe the man I blame for taking advantage of my mother, ruining her life, and then abandoning her, was the only one who made her feel safe.

I have this memory of being at the park with Momma and Uncle Ellis when I was really little. The new park. I was flying through the sunlight on a swing. It was a good day, warm, not quite hot. Momma was smiling even with Uncle Ellis there. Her hair was clean and her face bright. Maybe it was the sunlight, even the dark smudges under her eyes were gone.

She was happy, and I was free to play. So, I wasn't paying attention when that guy came up to them at the table. I still have no idea what made Uncle

Ellis mad. I don't know what the guy was saying, but his high-pitched sniveling made me stop pumping my legs and look over.

Right then I saw Uncle Ellis' hand move, heard the thunk as his knife hit the table. It was so fast I couldn't tell what happened. The guy started screaming, not high-pitched anymore. Deep and angry and surprised. When he pulled his hand away, his pinky stayed on the table.

My swing slowed down, but not fast enough. I thought I would throw up if I couldn't get off that swing. Not because of the finger that didn't belong there on the table. Because that's the first time I saw Uncle Ellis the way everyone else does, a monster in a human mask. After I saw him, I couldn't unsee him.

So right now, reading Momma's story, I'm thinking that cutting off Craig's ear seems more like something Uncle Ellis would do, not Dad.

I think about where Dad must be right now. What he must be doing. I wonder, if I looked hard, could see what Momma saw? I wonder if it is anywhere still in there. Or if it ever was.

Ruby Bell   2/22/1995

I asked Carrie if I could borrow her lip gloss. She looked at me funny but handed it to me. I left my hair down today, even though it was driving me crazy, tickling my face all day. Three different girls told me I looked pretty. They said it like they were surprised.

I wanted to run to the park after school to see if he was there. But Carrie was already tripping out on me, so I tried to act normal, even though I haven't felt normal in days.

I was so frustrated when he wasn't there. We only had like an hour and a half before we had to be back at the school for Sandy to pick us up after Marissa's basketball game. I just wanted to see him again, to see what he looked like. Maybe I only imagined him.

He came, though. I know he comes to the park all the time, but this time I felt like he came to see me. He wore a flannel shirt, but not baggy jeans like other guys wear. I hate those. He wears 501s.

He didn't talk to me. I didn't care.

He looked over Eric's shoulder at me once. I didn't care what he was doing there, who he was talking to, or why. I saw him. He saw me. And he walked behind me on his way back to his truck. He flicked my hair. It was nothing. Just his usual joking around. It was enough.

Ruby Bell _____ 3/13/1995

I skipped school again on Friday. He came.

He acted kind of shy when he first sat down. He kept looking around, like he thought someone was going to walk up and see us. But it was too early in the morning for anyone else to be there. I wasn't worried.

He asked me how old I am. He didn't look up when I told him I'm only fourteen. I think it bothered him. He asked me why I kept coming to the park.

I said, "To see you."

He told me I don't need to get in trouble at school. I told him I don't care about school. He said I should. He said he'd feel guilty if I got in trouble at school for him. So, I asked him when else I could see him.

He was sitting next to me, straddling the bench with his hands in the pockets of his flannel jacket. He bounced his knees like he was nervous. I thought he was going to say something, the way he took a deep breath. But he let it out slow, like he changed his mind.

I had to make him talk. I kept asking him what was wrong. Finally, he said he didn't think I should see him. That we don't need to see each other. So, I asked him if he didn't like me. But I already knew the answer.

And he said, "Ahhh man. You can't ask me that. That's not fair."

I slid closer to him on the bench, slid my hands inside his jacket around his ribs and up his back. I wedged myself between his legs. I felt his breathing, quick explosions going in, slow and shaky coming out. I told him I didn't care what he said, I didn't care what anybody said, I wanted to see him.

And then I kissed him. He gave in for a second and kissed me back. It was slow and soft, and he groaned deep in his throat. And then he put his hands on each side of my face to pull me away. He told me I needed to go back to school. But he was smiling. He said he wanted me to do good in school. So, I told him he needed to figure out another way for us to see each other. I said it kind of pouty.

He shook his head, like he thought it was funny that I was being a brat. But he was thinking of a way. I could just tell.

He kissed me on the forehead, and he held me there with his hand under my hair, holding the back of my head. He took a deep breath before he let me go. Then he told me to get back to school.

I felt his eyes on my back until I turned the corner at the end of the road.

Ruby Bell   3/21/1995

I've skipped school three more times. But he hasn't been at the park. It's the only place I know to find him.

But today, Marissa had a track meet. We were at the park, and Carrie sat down at the picnic table. There wasn't enough room for me. That's why I didn't see it first. I had to stand. But Carrie sees everything. She asked me if I did it. She had to lean sideways so I could look past her.

My name was carved into the top of the table. Right where we sat when I kissed him.

Ruby Bell   4/3/1995

I told Mrs. Patterson off today. Sort of.

She's sitting over there at her desk, and I'm writing in my journal, just waiting for this class to be over.

She got my attendance report. I guess I should be sorry. But I still can't figure out why. Who cares if I go to school? I used to be so scared to get in trouble. I just wanted to be good and not make anyone mad. But now I really don't think anyone will do anything to me. Not my social worker. Not Sandy. Not even Mrs. Patterson.

They can't really care about me. I mean let's be honest, the only time Sandy ever really punishes anyone is when they're bothering her personally. And Mrs. Patterson is probably just disappointed because I'm not giving her any dirt on Sandy.

I asked Mrs. Patterson flat out why she even cared what I did. She blinked and shook her head a little, like I slapped her.

She finally said, "Because I care about you Ruby."

Yeah right. Like I'm stupid.

I told her I knew she didn't care about me. I told her Carrie told me all about how she's just out to get Sandy. I said I knew she only keeps me around to help her catch Sandy doing something wrong.

And she told me, "Ruby, that's not true at all. I care about you," blah blah blah, "Sandy has a history..." But she didn't finish that sentence.

I'm sure she was about to say something really bad about Sandy. And I wouldn't be surprised by anything she said. I mean, it's probably true. Especially after what Craig did.

Then she went back to "I care about you Ruby. I just want to make sure you're safe."

She was pretty surprised when I told her how I know she thinks it's her job and everything, but she CAN'T make sure I'm safe. I told her that in the real world, where I live, you can't keep people safe by filling out forms and filing paperwork and telling people to write down their feelings. I was pretty surprised I said that too. But it's true.

And she said, "Ruby, it IS my job to report it to CPS when I suspect a child is being harmed."

And I asked her what good that was supposed to do when CPS put us there in the first place.

She took a deep breath and changed the subject. Probably because she knows I'm right. She said we weren't talking about her, we were talking about me. And she wanted to know what had gotten into me.

I didn't answer her, so we just stared at each other. For a long time. Long enough that I started wondering if maybe I was wrong. Maybe she really did care about me. Maybe she really wanted to know. Then I started feeling bad, and I looked away.

She asked me if I was okay. If there was something she needed to know about, or something I needed to talk about.

This would have been the time to tell her about Craig. But seriously, why? What could she do besides make it worse? Anyways, someone who really cares about me already handled it.

I told her I'm fine.

And of course, she wanted to know where I went when I wasn't in class. I told her I was in the girls' bathroom, having panic attacks. That worked. She told me she wanted me to come to her office when I started feeling overwhelmed.

I said, "Yes, Ma'am." And she didn't ask me another question about it.

She even excused my absences. Now I really am sorry, but I'm still not sure why.

"Did you know there used to be a park down old Mission Hill Road?" I ask Colby the next morning.

"No." He's lying on his bedroom floor throwing a ball in the air and catching it just before it lands on his head. "I didn't think there was anything down that road since they closed down that junkyard."

"We should go check it out."

He looks at me and squinches up his face like he's trying to decide whether it's worth the effort.

"What else is there to do?" I ask.

"Read. Be lazy. Write college application essays," he answers. And they're all good choices.

"You can do all that when the sun goes down."

We have to walk to the park because Aunt Rita doesn't want Colby using all the gas in her car. Which is funny to me because Grandma gave him that gas money for going to the store. But I guess it's her car, even though he fixed it.

I'm not sure exactly where the park is or was. We keep walking, and Colby is trying to get me to give up. He keeps asking me how I heard about this park. I knew he was going to ask. I had a lie all ready to go. I was going to say I saw it on an old map at the library.

But then, I don't know why, but I kind of tell him the truth. "Mrs. Patterson said Momma and Dad met down there."

After that, he shuts up about going home. And then we come up on it. It's just an overgrown field, not much different than the rest of the scrub land around it. Just a little greener. The cedar trees are barely bush size, not tree size. I know for sure it's the park when I see the rusty pipe fence. This park is tiny compared to the new one.

Colby slips between the fence rails, but I go to the space where the gate used to be. The picnic table is still there. The frame is one piece, made from pipes just like the fence. One of the benches is rotted through, and the two broken ends hang from their rusty bolts. The tabletop is there.

And so is Momma's name. Ruby. Four letters. He didn't make any curved lines, just a series of angles and triangles.

Colby comes up and stands next to me.

"Dude, that's your mom."

"Yeah." For a tiny second, I wish I hadn't brought him along. He isn't ruining it or anything, but I feel guilty. Here I have this proof that my parents kind of cared about each other. Even as messed up as they were. Colby doesn't even have a name to say out loud, because I haven't told him what I know.

Then again, he has something I don't. Colby at least has hope of meeting his dad one day. And I have the certainty that I'll never see my mother again.

I stand there looking at that carving for a long time. Colby stays quiet and lets me think. I love him so much because he doesn't try to talk at the wrong time.

I wait for something to click inside of me. I'm waiting for that magic moment that you read about in books when everything makes sense. But it just isn't coming.

"I want this," I tell Colby, and I start pulling on the board that has her name on it. The wood is gray and crumbly, and it only takes a few good tugs before I hear the cracking sound.

"Be careful," Colby tells me and edges me out of the way. "You need to pull on it by the bolts, so you don't break the part with her name."

He reaches under the board on one end, gives it a whack, and the board comes loose. Then he pries it up and wrenches the other end loose. It's pretty long but I don't care. I'm carrying it back.

About halfway home, Colby takes it from me to give me a rest.

"What're you going to do with this?" he asks.

"I don't know. I don't want Dad to see it," I say. "Do you think I can cut it down to just the part with her name? Then I can hide it somewhere."

"I can do it for you," he says.

I don't have to tell him why I want to hide it from Dad. I'm not the only one who doesn't talk about Momma. No one does. Especially not Dad.

Ruby Bell   4/7/1995

Sandy said Carrie and I could stay at the Easter Festival until it ended if we helped her with the little ones during the day. I watched the parade holding Caroline's hand with Brice, a chunky two-year-old, on my hip. Then we took them on the kiddy rides at the carnival. By six, Carrie and I were on our own, in town and free to do what we wanted until eleven o'clock.

I've never stayed at the carnival before. I know all the kids from school always go. It always seemed kind of like a party. Normally that would be enough to make me dizzy. I think if I hadn't been so excited to see Jimmy, I might have freaked out completely.

But I wanted to see him. I wanted him to see me. I wanted to see his face when he saw how Carrie fixed my hair, sprayed and feathered in a wave over my forehead. After Sandy left, we went into the bathroom at the Civic center, and Carrie showed me how to put on eyeliner the way she does.

Then we hung out with Eric and Rita, who was really starting to show now that she was almost six months pregnant. She's having a girl this time, and she dropped out of school for good. She's going to move in with the baby's daddy. I heard she's going to leave her first baby, the little boy, with her mom. But she hasn't told me that part, so I don't know for sure. I'm not going to ask.

We found Eric and walked around the carnival. None of us had money for rides. We stopped to talk to people, some people from school, some from the park, some I've never met. Eric asked if he could bum a cigarette from this guy who got mad because Eric took two. Eric just laughed at him, lit one and put the other one behind his ear.

I guess Carrie's good at sneaking out, because I sleep in the same room with her, and I've never heard her leave. But she was making plans for this guy to pick her up at eleven thirty. She didn't even ask me if I wanted to go, and I'm glad because that wasn't even enough time for Sandy to fall asleep after we got home.

She was still talking to that guy, flirting with him, when I saw Jimmy.

He was wearing 501s and his flannel shirt. I saw him before he saw me. He was walking with an older guy I've never seen before and there was a girl between them. She had yellow hair, fake and bright, and I could see a greenish tattoo, some kind of flower, on her chest. I let out my breath when I saw her take the other guy's hand.

Jimmy had to feel me staring. I swear I felt it when his eyes touched me.

The three of them walked up to us and made sort of a half circle around our group. Then our little group unfolded and let them in. Jimmy didn't speak to me, but he never took his eyes off me. He asked Eric about a party out by the lake.

He said "You should go," to the guy, but it was like he was saying it only to me.

Everyone wanted to go, and Rita said she could take us. But Carrie was the last person to fit into the back of Rita's Grand Am, and then it was too full for me to fit. Eric flipped the front seat back, got in and closed the passenger door. He smiled and shrugged through the window while they pulled out and left me behind.

I stood there under the lights of the parking lot for a minute. Not even a minute. Just a few seconds. I was thinking how stupid it was to come to the festival. So stupid to trust people who don't even like me. So stupid to think they would want me to go with them to a party. I was going to be left at the carnival, all alone, until eleven. All those thoughts went through my mind in those few seconds.

Then I felt Jimmy's hand on my wrist. He asked me if I was going. And I tried to be cool and tell him I didn't want to go, that I didn't know anyone there.

He said, "You know me."

And I felt my face get hot, and I kept my eyes on the ground. He said we didn't have to stay at the party if I didn't want to. He moved his hand down, laced his fingers with mine, and pulled me toward him. I kept my eyes down. I rubbed my thumb along his and told him I didn't want to go to the party.

He didn't make me look at him. He just pushed my hair back behind my ear and asked where I wanted to go. I told him I didn't care, I just wanted to be with him. He groaned and tried to let my hand go, but I held on. He said he had to go to the party, at least for a little bit.

I said okay, I'd go, and I let him lead me to his truck, to the driver's side door. I got in and sat in the middle of the seat waiting. He didn't get in right away. He looked me over, then he groaned again. He said I had to quit looking at him like that.

Then when he got in, he kissed me. A real kiss. Long and hard, like he couldn't help himself. I didn't know where the party was, but I knew we weren't going there first.

He turned off the highway onto an old gravel road. His headlights swung over a trailer house and finally stopped on a camper, one of those kinds that go on the back of a truck. It was sitting up on cement blocks.

He turned off the truck, turned off the lights, and sat there with both hands on the steering wheel. I didn't want him to change his mind, so I didn't talk. I tried to be still. Then I worried he'd change his mind if I gave him too much time, so I scooted closer to him, and told him I was getting cold.

That's all it took. He kissed me again, there in the seat of the truck. I thought we wouldn't even make it into the camper. But we did.

He helped me into the bunk and then climbed up behind me. I laid back on the mattress where the sheet had come loose from one corner. I didn't know what to do, and I started getting scared again. I started thinking maybe I'd made a mistake. I was cold, even with my jeans and jacket on, and I didn't want to take them off. A queasiness came over me. A sick feeling, like something really bad was about to happen.

Maybe he can just feel what I'm feeling. Is that possible? Because instead of making any more moves, he just flopped down beside me. And he said he was sorry. He said he really wanted to do this, but he couldn't.

I didn't answer him. I didn't want to say I didn't want to do this either. I didn't want him to think I never wanted to, just because I wasn't ready right then. I told him I was still cold.

He slid his arm under my head and pulled me close to him. Then he reached over me for the blanket.

He said, "We can't see each other. I don't know what's wrong with me."

I told him I was going to see him one way or the other. I said he might think I'm crazy, but I needed to see him. Because I don't want to go back to the way I was before I met him, barely hanging on and about to be swallowed whole by a fat old man like Craig. It was just a matter of time. When that old man touched me, I just wanted to die. And now, Craig is scared of me.

I turned on my side and propped myself up on one elbow to look down at him. I thought about the weeks I waited to see him again, and I knew this chance wouldn't come around again soon. I told him I belonged to him, and if I couldn't be with him I didn't know what I'd do.

I kissed him again, and this time there wasn't any sick feeling in my stomach. This time I couldn't get my jacket and pants off fast enough.

It hurt like crazy. But when it was over, something inside me, something agitated and shrill had gone silent.

Then, later, when we were at the party, I felt like everyone could tell, just by looking at me, that I was not the same person. Even when he left me to go do whatever he does with people, I still felt safe.

CHAPTER 11

I don't know whether to cry or throw up. My mother was a child, throwing herself at a grown man. There's a drawing of Dad on the next page. It's on regular notebook paper, so I wasn't expecting it. There's some kind of magic in her sketch, because I know right away that it's him. But the man on the paper doesn't look anything like Dad looks now. Momma's spent a lot of time on this. I can tell because there are eraser marks and smudges in lots of places.

I realize I've never seen an actual picture of Dad from back then. We don't have pictures of anything. I'd like to think Momma made him look younger and more handsome than he was. Then it wouldn't be so horrible to know what he turned into.

I'm thinking so hard about Dad, and I don't hear Uncle Ellis' truck when it pulls up. But I hear the radio get loud when the door opens. I hear Dad talk to him, then shut the door.

I barely have time to get the binder closed and under the cushion. Then I slide down on the bench and close my eyes just as he pulls the door open.

"What the fuck is this?" he yells, and I pretend to wake up. "What're you doing sleeping with that tree plugged in? You'll burn this place to the ground. Where did you get that piece of shit anyway?"

"At the thrift shop," I say, pretending to wake up, ignoring his other questions.

He doesn't unplug it. He just flops down on the bench across the table from me and rubs his eyes.

"Is there anything to eat?" he asks.

"There's bologna," I tell him. "You want a sandwich?"

I don't wait for him to answer; I just get up and make him one. He's so skinny. His knees look like knots on his rope thin legs.

I wonder how I feel about my father now that I know how much she really loved him. My mother was a child. All my life I wished he had left her alone. He ruined her life, and he hasn't done much better for me. He means nothing to me. I have so many reasons to hate him. But I don't want to watch this thing he's doing to himself.

I pour a glass of milk and hand it to him. He looks at me, surprised and maybe a little grateful. But that might be me imagining things. After I give him his sandwich, I lay back down on my side of the camper and pretend to fall asleep again, because I don't want to listen to him. Then, eventually I do fall asleep.

He's still on the bench, asleep in his clothes, when I wake up the next morning. His hat's on the floor, and his arm is over his eyes. The sandwich has one bite out of it, and it's sitting on the table under the Christmas tree like a present.

That's the trouble with breaks from school. Eventually Dad comes home, and then we're stuck in this tiny box together. When he's home, I have to ask him before I go anywhere, and half the time he says no. Normally I just read or draw when I'm trapped here. But this time I can't bring myself to read anything with Momma's journal waiting to be finished.

I lay there thinking about sneaking out. I lay there so long I start wondering why I'm so scared to ask him about Momma. Then I wonder what I'd ask him if I wasn't scared. Maybe I'm scared for him to ruin my memories. He's so much shit, he can't help himself. He'll ruin it by insulting her without realizing it. That's why I'm not asking him anything.

Thankfully, Colby knocks on the door. He's just as bored as I am and looking to get away from his mom. I can tell he was hoping to hang out in the camper, because when he sees Dad, he shrinks a little and backs away from the door.

I slip my feet into my shoes, grab my hoody and step outside. Then I stand there for a second to make sure Dad hasn't woken up.

We used to sit in the car before it was fixed. Back when it was impossible to go anywhere in it. Now that the car is running, it doesn't seem like a place to hang out. It's too full of potential. If we got in that car now, Aunt Rita would come out and want to know where we planned on going.

So we go to the burn pit behind the farm house where, a long time ago, someone drug up big flat topped rocks to sit on. Maybe it was my grandparents, or maybe that was back when Grandma let Dad have people over. Maybe they had parties back there, but no one uses it now. It's like a Jennings version of Stonehenge.

Those rocks are hard and cold, so a couple years ago, Colby and I carried plastic lawn chairs home from the Dollar Store. The wind has blown them into the cedar more than a few times, and they're faded now from the sun, but we still use them. We finally quit asking Rita to let us build fires back there though. She says we'll burn everyone's house down. So if it's cold, sometimes we take blankets out there with us.

"When did your dad get home?" Colby asks.

"Last night," I say. "Uncle Ellis dropped him off."

"It's weird how you call him Uncle Ellis."

I've never thought about it before. That's how Momma talked to me about him, so that's what I call him. But I don't answer Colby, I just nod. It is weird.

"Where'd you hide that board?" he asks.

"In the farmhouse. I guess we'll have to wait for Dad to leave before we can cut it."

"Who carved that? Do you know?"

"Yeah. Dad did it."

"So why don't you want him to see it?"

I search my mind for a lie. All these unspoken things are so comfortable, left where they are. They bind me to Colby. He knows so much, shares so much of my history that I don't have to talk to him about it. But if I keep this new thing, this new version of our shared history to myself, it could change everything between us.

"I have Momma's journal." It just busts out of me.

"Her journal? What journal?"

"She kept a journal when she was my age. Mrs. Patterson had it. She gave it to me. That's how I know about the table."

"Why would Mrs. Patterson have your mom's journal?" He's staring at me, because this is a really big deal to someone just finding out about it. I'm staring at the ground. "What's in it?"

"A lot of stuff." I roll a stick under my shoe, then reach down to pick it up. "She wrote about meeting Dad."

Colby is silent now. Probably thinking about what else might be in there.

"It's crazy, Colby, reading all of that," I say. "It's like we kind of know what happened back then, but reading her words, when she's talking about Dad and your mom, it's like... it's crazy. We don't know them. We don't know them at all."

"I don't really want to know them, Jade," he says. "Maybe your mom, but

135

not mine. Not your dad. They fuck everything up."

I laugh at that. It's true.

"She used to draw," I say. "She was way better than me."

"So how in the world did she end up here?" he asks the question that has echoed in my head for as long as I can remember. This is how Colby is the other half of me. He's seen it all, imagined how it looks to me, and wondered the same thing I have. He never asked me because he knows I don't have any more answers than he does.

"It's kind of starting to make sense now," I tell him. "It's still messed up, don't get me wrong."

"Yeah," he says, "You and I both know she never belonged here. I don't care what she wrote, that's never going to change."

"We don't belong here either, Colby," I tell him. "I know that too."

"Can I see it?" he asks. "The journal…"

"I want you to see it," I tell him. "She talks about your mom. Your dad."

He turns his eyes to me. "Did she know him?"

"No, I don't think so. But she knew who he was. She'd heard of him. His last name was Dempsey. But that's all there is in there."

"Just a last name? Why just a last name?"

I close my eyes. I don't want to be the one. But there is no one else.

"I think he was a teacher at the high school," I finally say, even though my teeth are clenched, like they're mad at me for being such a big mouth.

Colby hasn't taken his eyes off me, but I can't look at him.

"He was a math teacher," I say.

And then there is more silence.

Finally, he laughs. "I've heard that you know? Kids at school used to tell me my dad was a pervert. But I didn't know his name. I mean who was I going to ask?"

I never knew people teased him about his dad. This seems impossible to me. How could there be anything about Colby I don't know?

"What's that called where they don't know if you learn stuff from your parents, or if it's genetic?" he asks.

"Nature vs. nurture?"

"Yeah, that. So I guess math is nature?"

I laugh out loud. I'm so relieved he's not pissed at me. "I've been thinking the same thing!"

And then we're quiet again, because math might be a good thing, but getting a student pregnant isn't. I guess I understand why he never told me what he knew about his dad. I keep everything about my mother to myself. But now I have to rethink everything about Colby and his mystery dad.

Colby and I need to put our bets on a theory that doesn't involve nature or nurture. But I also hope we got some magical something from our missing parents that'll be like a passport out of here. Something that'll help us fit in when we get where we're going.

"I'll let you read every word of it when I get finished. I promise." I hope I can keep this promise, but I'm not so sure.

We sit for a while longer, then he gets up and walks around the farmhouse where what's left of the tool shed is leaning on two warped posts. He comes back with a rusty hacksaw, and I get up and follow him into the farmhouse.

The board from the picnic table is only about eight inches long when he's done trimming it. I leave it inside the farmhouse. I'll hide it under my bench cushion later. Just not while Dad's home.

When Colby says he needs to go to the library to check his email and search for scholarship applications, I let him go alone. I know he's going to search the Internet to find out more about Mr. Dempsey, who taught math at Oak Grove in the 90's. I feel like he'll want to be alone while he does that.

Christmas comes and goes, but I still have that tree up because I like the lights.

Dad's sick. He has been for days. I start out pissed at him for being stupid

138

and getting himself sick. And I think he's a giant baby because he's so helpless, needing me to get him water, asking me to walk to the store to get him medicine for his stomach.

I wonder where he'd be if I were the one sick. Nowhere. That's where he'd be. I'd have Colby to help me and that's it.

He finally quit throwing up, but the whole camper reeks from the last time he used the bathroom. He has sores all in his mouth, and he can barely drink anything. He looks gross. But I sort of feel bad for him. He manages to get himself up into the bunk, and I bring him more milk because that seems to help the most. And then he hands the half-empty glass back and turns away from me.

Later, he's shaking the camper, and I don't know if he's going to be sick again or if he's crying.

I keep reminding myself that he always does this. Just because I read Momma's journal, and she liked him for some reason doesn't make him a different person. Seeing a slight glimmer of a slight possibility that he might, maybe, have been a decent human being to my mother, even though he was actually a pedophile, isn't enough. It just isn't.

If he's up there crying and feeling sorry for himself, it's for the things he did to himself. He's not up there crying and feeling sorry for the things he did, and still does, to everyone else.

Still I'm relieved when he finally manages to eat the whole bowl of ramen noodles I made for him. He's probably going to be okay, but it won't be long until he's back to his usual irritated self. I wash his dirty bowl, then tell him I'm going to see Colby and slip out the door before he can say no.

I hate it when he comes home like this. It takes days for him to get better, and the whole time, I'm afraid to leave him alone. I just know I'll come back and he'll be dead up there in that bunk. I'm tired of worrying. I'm ready for school to start back. Ready for Dad to call Uncle Ellis or Harmon and get back to whatever business they have with each other.

I'm sitting in Colby's room when I hear the sound of an engine. I peek out the window to see that dusty red Ford rambling up the road in the orange light of the sunset. Uncle Ellis doesn't get out. He just honks. He's already pushing his luck with Grandma by driving onto her property. Dad must have called him. He must have been feeling just as trapped as I was.

It's almost ten when I go back to the camper and plug in my tree. It's not too cold outside so I open the windows to get rid of the smell Dad left behind. Then I pull out Momma's binder.

Ruby Bell   5/1/1995

I don't even have to ask permission when I leave the house at night. Sandy just lets me go. I think she knows about what Craig did. I think she's afraid I'll tell on him. One night she kind of got onto me for not locking the door when I got home, but that's all she ever said.

Jimmy wants me to finish school. So we spend all our time in his camper.

He takes me home by eleven so I can get up in the morning.

I think, finally, everything might just turn out okay.

Ruby Bell   5/5/1995

Mrs. Patterson saw a hickey on my neck the other morning. I could tell she was embarrassed to bring it up, but she asked me about it.

I was filing for half the class period. SAT scores came in. She sat at her desk watching me. She asked if I had a boyfriend, and I said yes. I couldn't think of any reason to lie. She asked if he went to school at Oak Grove, and I told her he was out of school. Her drawn on eyebrows went up when she heard that. Then she asked where I met him, and I didn't want her to know I hang out at that park, so I told her he's Rita Jennings' brother.

She blinked. And blinked again. And the whole time her eyebrows were so high, her forehead was nothing but rows of wrinkles.

She said, "James Jennings?"

I said, "Jimmy."

She asked if I knew how old he is. I said yes and asked her why that mattered. And then she told me that I'm fourteen, as if I don't already know that. So I rolled my eyes, I couldn't help it. And I told her that I'm about to be fifteen.

She closed her eyes for a second, took a deep breath. She had the nerve to ask me if I was having sex with "James Jennings." Hearing her say it out loud was kind of shocking. It sounded so nasty. I told her that was kind of a personal question.

And she said she needed to know. Because if I'm having sex with him, she'll have to report him to the authorities. She said I'm a child, and he's an adult. Slowly, it started to make sense, what she was trying to say. And I told her it wasn't like that. That she didn't understand. I'm not a child. She asked me if Sandy knew I was dating him, but I wasn't about to tell her anything else.

I told her, "I'm not dating him, and I'm not having sex with him, okay?"

She backed off after that. I know Sandy and Craig are just trying to keep themselves out of trouble. But I think Mrs. Patterson is afraid of making me mad for some reason.

So then, when I got home, Sandy said she wanted to talk to me.

She was all, "I've been doing my level best to let you handle your own business, but now I have that counselor calling me about you…"

I was so mad. All I could think is how I will never tell Mrs. Patterson anything ever again. And Sandy was telling me it was my fault for going to school with hickeys on my neck. She said it seemed like I was trying to get everyone in trouble on purpose.

So I started crying. And I told her it's no one's business but mine. And I said I hated Mrs. Patterson, and I hated Sandy most of all. And Jimmy is the only person who isn't trying to use me, for welfare money or to try to get dirt on someone else. He's the only person who really cares about me, and they just can't stand it because they can't push me around like they used to.

And she said, "I'm not trying to use you, you little bitch, I'm trying not to lose my husband and my house."

And she said I was just mad because I couldn't fuck her husband so I had to go find a child molesting drug dealer and cause even more problems for her.

And then she said, "Where do you think these little ones will go if I lose my license?"

I thought about Caroline in a new home with strangers. With city kids who are probably way meaner than Genesis. I felt the panic coming, burning. I felt tears coming, and all of a sudden, I couldn't get enough air. I tried to fight it, but I knew I was going to throw up. And then I thought maybe if I threw up I'd feel better. Sometimes that works. So I ran to the bathroom and let it all out.

I stayed in the bathroom even after my stomach was empty. But Sandy won't let the kids use the bathroom in her room. I had to come out so they could use it. I didn't want to be at the house anymore, but I couldn't call Jimmy. He doesn't have a phone. All I could do was will him to know I needed him. But he never came.

When I went to my room, Carrie was in there, lying on her bed. She just looked at me like I was crazy, like she does every time I freak out. I climbed into my bed and cried, but I cried quietly because I really didn't want Carrie yelling at me.

<u>Ruby Bell</u>   5/10/1995

Jimmy picked me up from school yesterday and I told him all about what happened. I thought he would say it was all going to be okay, and he would fix it, like he did with Craig. But he didn't. He just got quiet. And then he took me straight home.

I kept asking him what was wrong. He said nothing. He said he'd see me again soon. But that's not what it felt like. It felt like he was saying he couldn't see me again ever.

<u>Ruby Bell</u>   5/12/1995

Today I asked Mrs. Patterson if I could get my schedule changed, to quit being her aide. Even if it was just for the last few weeks of school. I told her I never wanted to speak to her again.

She tried to talk to me. She told me I couldn't change my schedule. I told her I was going to kill myself if I couldn't see Jimmy. She said that I didn't mean it, but if I kept saying that she would need to have me sent to a facility where I could get help.

I do mean it though.

So I asked why it was easier to put me in a mental ward than to let me see the one person in the world I care about. The one person in the world who cares about me.

She said because of the law. But why would I care about the law? I can promise you, the law has never cared one bit about me.

<u>Ruby Bell</u>   <u>5/18/1995</u>

I haven't heard from Jimmy in almost a week. So I missed the bus on purpose and walked to his camper. He wasn't there. I sat on the step to wait for him. It was already starting to get dark when his mom came out of her house and saw me there.

She's a scary old woman with a mean mean face and I know she doesn't like me. Jimmy's never even introduced me to her, but I've seen her. She just shakes her head when she sees me, and Jimmy rushes me inside the camper if she's outside.

She finally raised the window and yelled, "He ain't home. He's off with Ellis. No tellin' when he'll be back. You go on now."

I didn't answer her. I just got up and started walking back down the road. The light of day was completely gone by the time I came to the corner store.

I finally got to see what Ellis Hoyle looks like. When I came up to the store, he pushed through the glass door thumping a hard pack of Marlboro Reds. I guessed it was Ellis Hoyle because Jimmy was waiting for him in a big red truck. I wanted to run over to Jimmy, but I didn't. There's something about Ellis Hoyle. I don't like him. So I stayed in the dark, outside the circle of light coming from the building, until they drove away.

When they were gone, I went inside the store and called Sandy.

She was so mad when she got there, she slapped me. I think she was trying to get me to go crazy like I did the other night. She probably wanted an excuse to call my social worker and say I was out of control and have me put in a facility.

And I don't know why I didn't lose it. I have been trying to figure that out.

Once, when I first came to Sandy's house, I was only about eleven or twelve, I was outside with the water hose on. I think I was washing out trash cans or something, and I accidentally ran the hose over this open electric socket on the side of the house. It took me a second to realize what the feeling was. The electricity was running upstream and into my arm. It was a horrible sickening feeling. And it left my whole arm numb for a long time after.

I don't know what it was about Ellis Hoyle, but that is exactly how I felt after seeing him.

I sit for a long time after reading this last page. I put my fingers on her words. On Uncle Ellis' name, where she describes seeing him for the first time. All of this about Dad is so typical, so much like the crap on those shows Aunt Rita's always watching.

But Uncle Ellis. His presence winds through my memories of Momma like one of those thorny vines that grow up and cover entire trees and telephone poles. Her first time seeing him is hidden here in these pages, it was significant, even then.

I close the journal and slide it under my cushion. I unplug my tree and finally manage to fall asleep.

I want to finish reading the journal before I see Mrs. Patterson again. I don't like the idea of her knowing everything in it when I don't. So the next morning, as soon as I drift up out of sleep, even before the sky is lit, the journal is the first thing on my mind. I plug in my tree and pull the binder out again.

<u>Ruby Bell</u> <u>5/25/1995</u>

I gave up on trying to see Jimmy. Now I'm trying to get it through my head that people just aren't allowed to be that happy. I still won't speak to Mrs. Patterson. It's pathetic the way she keeps trying.

I keep my head down, and I keep writing and avoid looking at her. Sometimes I cry in her office, but I don't let her see. She'll just want to know why, and it isn't worth talking about.

I get so tired, and I really don't understand people. How do they keep on? They just keep getting up every day and struggling through life, and I don't understand how they find the energy. And I can't understand why? What do they really get in the end?

I'm just so tired.

I don't know how Carrie knew I was pregnant. I didn't even know. I mean my boobs are growing but I'm fourteen, they're supposed to be growing. And I never pay attention to my period. I've been so tired and thinking about Jimmy so much, I forgot all about that.

I guess since I'm so skinny, my little pot belly looks out of place. I was putting on my pajamas one night when Carrie yelled it out. "You're fucking pregnant!"

It was the weirdest thing, like a flood of warmth ran over me. I knew it was true. I had Jimmy's baby inside of me. Like magic.

I finished putting on my pajamas and told Carrie to be quiet. Then I turned off the light and lay there in the dark, smiling to myself. I don't know how pregnant I am. I haven't seen Jimmy in a month and a half. So at least that pregnant. Probably more. I couldn't sleep thinking about what it meant. I wonder what he'll say when I tell him. I wonder how I'll even find him to tell him. It doesn't matter. I imagine Jimmy's face when he sees me again. Especially if he doesn't see me until I'm really showing. Or maybe after the baby is already born.

I imagine our baby, what he'll look like. I hope he has Jimmy's smile.

I feel so sorry for my mother. She had to know that my dad used her and ditched her, didn't she? I mean she has to be writing this insanity as some kind of comfort for herself. I feel guilty for thinking that about her. I should be happy she wanted me.

She thought I was going to be a boy. I wonder if she was sad when I turned out to be a girl. I don't know if I have Dad's smile. There's barely anything left of his teeth. And he doesn't smile anymore.

Ruby Bell   7/14/1995

I wasn't going to tell anyone I'm pregnant. But Carrie told Sandy and now I have to go to the doctor. And my social worker needs to meet with me.

I guess Sandy can just get rid of me now. I think they have homes just for pregnant girls, but they're all in Austin. I'm not as scared of getting beat up in a home for pregnant girls. I don't think they'll be as mean there. But then again, getting beat up while I'm pregnant would be a whole lot worse.

I don't want to leave without telling Jimmy. But Sandy says if I tell anyone who the daddy is, Jimmy might end up in jail. She's just worried she'll end up in trouble because of me. But I don't want the other girls to have to move. So I keep telling them I don't know who it was. That it was someone I met at the carnival. I keep telling them that I didn't even ask his name.

CHAPTER 12

The next page is a big piece of sketch paper, folded in half. I unfold it, and the carnival scene that Momma drew fills the whole page. There's a Super Loop in the back, a fun house and a carousel. The front of the funhouse is a clown face, and the mirror maze is his mouth. The light bulbs on the carousel, on the Fun Slide, on everything, are all shaded and smudged and drawn with so much detail, the gray drawing looks like it's lit up and glowing.

There are paths between the corndog stands, and the ticket booths and the ring toss games. But there are only two people. A boy and a girl, a man and a woman? Honestly, it's a man and a girl. I didn't see them at first. They are wrapped around each other on the top floor of the funhouse, in the eye of the clown.

This sketch must have taken hours, days, weeks.

I almost tip the journal off the table when Colby knocks. I get up and open the door, not bothering to even close the binder now that he knows about it. But he doesn't come in. His eyes are wide open, and he's looking at me like he has some kind of bad news to break, and I can't imagine what it is. The usual things run through my mind. The police are here. Dad was arrested. Dad is dead.

Then I look behind him, and I'm so not prepared for this. Sheila's standing right behind him. My mind trips and tumbles all over itself. I'm humiliated and scared and wondering what in the world brought her out here, and how she knew where to find me, and is she going to fire me now that she knows how I live.

The look on her face is almost as bad as Colby's. She's looking like she really wishes she hadn't come.

We all stand there for the longest time, because they're waiting for me to say something, and I cannot get any words to come through the horror I'm feeling. And then I do the unthinkable and ask her if she wants to come in. Colby looks at me like I've lost my mind, and Sheila, thank goodness, catches his look and says no.

"I uh…" Sheila starts, then starts again, "I wanted… I realized I don't have a phone number for you. Isn't that funny?" she laughs, and I try to smile back but it doesn't work. "After all this time, I don't have your number. So I uh.. I wanted to ask you if you could babysit on New Year's Eve. So Angie told me how to find you."

She seems to calm down once she gets that out. Like she gets herself back together once she can explain why she's here. And that helps me too. So I nod and take a deep breath, and finally I'm able to smile at her. And it's a real smile. I realize how much I miss Jathan and how much better I'll feel if I can just hang out with him for a while.

"I would love that, Mrs. Miller," I tell her.

"We'll be out late. I could drive you home after," she blinks, and I know she's working hard to keep from looking around, looking at the camper, "or you could spend the night."

"Whatever is easiest for you, Mrs. Miller. Or I can just walk home. It's usually getting dark by the time I get home anyway, so it's not a big deal."

She looks at me like I'm crazy, and I worry I might be making a bad impression on her. Like she might not trust my judgment if I think this is okay. So I stop talking.

"Why don't you bring clothes for a sleepover," she says and I'm watching her face to see if she's irritated with me. I feel so exposed, so off balance with her now that she knows where I live. How I live.

"Yes, ma'am," I tell her, and she tells me to be there at five. Then she smiles and says goodbye and goes back to her car. I let Colby in and close the camper door, but I watch Sheila out the window. She starts her car and sits there for a few seconds longer than I expected. I thought she'd peel out trying to get away, but she doesn't. She sits in her car and looks around for a while before she drives off slowly.

I turn around to see Colby staring at my mother's drawing.

"Holy shit!" he says. "This is incredible."

"I know," I say, and sit back down in front of the binder.

I go over this sketch, looking at it longer, taking in all the detail. Then I flip back to her other sketches. Colby has the same reaction that I did to the sketch of Dad.

"I've never seen a picture of him from back then," he says, "But if that's what he used to look like, he should be on one of those 'Don't Do Meth' posters."

I close the binder. Because maybe he looked like that. But most likely, Momma loved him so much, maybe she saw him better than he was.

"So are you just going to hole up in this camper until you've read that thing all the way through?" Colby asks me.

"What else is there to do?" I ask him.

"I don't know," he says, and sits down on the bench. He plays around with the flap on Momma's binder for a second. Then he says, "I found my dad."

I sit down too. It's more like I'm knocked down by what he just said.

"Found him….. like…. you talked to him?"

"Okay, no. But I have the number to where he works."

"When did you get it? This morning? How?"

"A couple of days ago. Internet," he says, and then he ducks his head and runs his hands through his hair. "He lost his teaching license or certificate or

153

whatever because of my mom. Because of me."

"How do you know that?"

"There was an investigation. It wasn't a big newspaper story like they do now on TV. It was a little article in the back of an old paper in the library. It didn't take long to find it. I mean, I had the general date range," he shrugs. "There wasn't anything about her getting pregnant in there. And I don't know what he did after he moved. Maybe he went back to college or something. But he's an engineer now at some fabrication plant in Temple."

"He's in Temple? Temple, Texas? Like an hour from here?" I ask. I never imagined he'd be so close, since Shelby's dad is all the way in Colorado, and the twins' dad went all the way back to Dallas. Men from around here would know better than to get involved with Rita Jennings. And the ones from out of town who made that mistake, got as far away from her as possible afterwards.

"What are you going to do?" I ask. I want to tell him it wasn't his fault his father lost his job, but I want to know the answer to this question more. "Are you going to call him at his work?"

"Should I?"

"What else is there to do?" I don't think there is anything else to do.

He nods. He's biting the side of his lip. He takes a deep breath and pulls his phone out of his pocket. It's a beat-up old flip phone on a month-to-month plan. But it's better than what I have, which is nothing, because I don't want to ask Dad to sign anything for me.

Colby has the number on a folded piece of notebook paper that he sets out on the table. After he dials, he takes another deep breath, puts the phone up to his ear and locks eyes on me. I hold his gaze and try to think strong, brave thoughts for him.

"Um, yes.. Is Allen Dempsey available?" he says into the phone in his best mature professional voice, and then he waits. "Thank you."

I'm holding my breath. It feels like Colby leaves me when he takes his eyes off me. I know it means Mr. Dempsey is on the phone.

"Um, yes... Hello, is this Mr. Dempsey? Allen Dempsey? Um, yes... this is... I'm... My name is Colby Jennings." I think Colby waits for a second, to see if Mr. Dempsey figures it out on his own. But the silence goes on too long. "I'm Rita Jennings' son."

Colby nods a couple of times while he listens, as if his father can hear that. Then he says, "Yes, sir. I understand. Yes, Sir. I will. Okay. Okay. Thank you. Okay. Bye."

He flips his phone closed and lets out a deep breath. "He's going to call me when he gets off work. Around six or so."

"What else did he say?" I ask. "Was he surprised? Did he sound mad?"

"I can't tell. Not mad. Tired maybe? Or sad. I don't know." Colby flips his phone open and closed a few times, and I know it's going to be a long wait for six o'clock.

We stare at each other until I break the silence. "I cannot believe you just did that."

"I know."

"Your dad. You just talked to your actual father on the phone."

"I know."

"So what are we going to do until six?" I ask.

I know what I want to do. I want to read my mother's journal. But I'm not leaving him to wait for this phone call by himself.

He shrugs.

"Do you have any money? We could go to a movie."

"Yeah. I'll have to put gas in mom's car, though."

"Just like five dollars or so, right? Just enough to get to Fairview."

"I'll go ask."

While he's gone, I flip open the binder and start on the page after the carnival drawing.

I moved again. I couldn't get to my journal when I was in Saint Ann's. I only got to keep a few of my things when I went in, like my clothes and toothbrush. After a while, none of my clothes fit anymore anyway, I got so big when I was pregnant. I guess the idea is to leave the past behind. But now here I am, sitting in the middle of this apartment floor, taking what's left of my past out of these boxes.

It's strange, reading my journal from back then. It's funny how I kept putting my name and date across the top. Like I thought Mrs. Patterson was going to want to read it or something. After a while it was like I had to start with that, just to get the words flowing. Man, I'm glad she never read it. But having it helps so much. Because sometimes I forget what it was about Jimmy. Sometimes it just feels like a habit, missing him.

I guess Saint Ann's was better than being at Sandy's. They made us take parenting classes and made sure we went to the doctor and all that. And there was no drama like there was at Sandy's. No one at Saint Ann's yelled or ever got mad at me. But mostly, I feel like that's because I never had a chance to make a mistake. Everything was so scheduled and organized, every minute of the day.

Not that anyone would have cared enough to actually yell. The women who run the place go home to their real lives when their shift is over. The pregnant girls that live there are just a job to them.

But Jade and I are doing fine. I qualified for this program where I can live in a HUD apartment. So now I'm back in Oak Grove and back in school, and I live in my own place. Jade will be in the Early Head Start program, and I'll get a check and food stamps like Rita did, except I'm going to live by myself. I have a new social worker who'll come in and check on me all the time, and the landlord is going to make sure I'm home every night and not having parties.

I couldn't wait to get back to Oak Grove. I haven't seen Jimmy since that day at the gas station when he was in the truck with Ellis. I should have called out to him then. I feel so stupid for being scared.

I feel like a completely different person since that day. I don't even look the same. I just turned sixteen. My hair is longer, curlier and darker red. My boobs are bigger, but so is my butt. I'm kind of scared to see him again. Scared for him to see me. I wonder what he'll think of me now that I have stretch marks.

But I can't wait for him to see Jade. She's going to be six months old tomorrow. I don't know how I'll find him without anyone knowing. I guess I could go to the park, but I'm not taking Jade there. If I don't run into him soon, maybe I'll take her for a walk out to the camper. I just don't know about Jimmy's mom. I don't want her yelling at me in front of my baby.

Ruby Bell   8/26/1996

At Saint Ann's, there was a room set up as a daycare, and we took our babies there while we went to class. We all took turns working in the room, and classes never lasted long. So I've never been away from Jade for longer than an hour at a time since she was born.

That would have sounded crazy to me a year ago, before I had a baby of my own. But now, I feel sick just thinking about dropping her off at Early Head Start. I didn't even push her there in her stroller. I carried her there in my arms to get as much time with her as I could.

And then I cried so hard in the baby room that the old lady had to take Jade out of my arms. The younger lady walked me out into the hall.

I caught the look they gave each other, and I know what they were thinking. That I'm too young to be a mom. And maybe I am. But I think my baby is too young to be away from me for so long.

I walked to school with that horrible feeling that I just did something very wrong. I guess I feel guilty that I got into this program and came back here just so I could find Jimmy. And now Jade is in a daycare with mean old ladies who don't really care about her. I have to keep reminding myself that I want to find him for her. She needs more family than just me. I'm all she has in the world right now. And I'm not much.

And then my first day back at school wasn't anything like I thought it would be. First, I had to sit with Mrs. Patterson and work out my schedule. She looked happy to see me and sorry and sad all at the same time. I know it isn't her fault. Even if she hadn't called Sandy, I would have ended up at Saint Ann's. But I was still mad at her when I walked in.

I wanted to stay mad, but she asked me about Jade, and I couldn't help it, I started talking. She looked so relieved. I kept talking because she seemed to really care about how Jade hates peas and when she learned to roll over. And she asked me questions, and I realized how much I had bottled up inside of me. How proud I am of my baby.

I felt good when I left her office. Then I went out into the hall, feeling like I'd see people I knew, or get some kind of welcome. I guess I was just so alone at Saint Ann's that I imagined I had friends here. By the time I got to my second class, I remembered how it was when I left. I might recognize some of these faces, but I really didn't know a soul.

I found Carrie at lunch. She was at her table with the rest of her friends, and they were nice to me at first. But I'm so awkward, I answered their questions like a dork, so they quit talking to me. After a while they seemed to forget I was there. I did hear that Rita finally dropped out for good. Carrie said Rita was living with her boyfriend and both of her kids somewhere in town, but she didn't know exactly where.

It was such a relief to find out Rita didn't leave her little boy. I thought about that a lot right after Jade was born, when people were talking to me about adoption. I don't know how I could live if someone took her away from me. I think my mind would just shut down completely.

I couldn't wait to get out of my last class to get her. I took her home, fed her chicken and carrots and played with her on the floor until she fell asleep. Then I made a sandwich and ate it by myself at the table.

It seems too quiet, alone in my apartment after so much time in places with so many people. I don't know what to do with myself. I have a couple of books that I've already read. I guess I'll need to take time at lunch to go to the library tomorrow.

Colby comes back and looks at me still in my pajamas.

"Are you wearing that?" he asks.

"No," I make a face at him and get up. I pull a pair of jeans out of the box on the shelf over the window and go into the tiny bathroom to change. When I come out he isn't in the camper. He's already in the car, waiting for me.

I can tell he's going to be all pissy while he waits for the call, and I don't blame him. I just pretend not to notice. I'm thinking about my mother now anyway. I didn't know she had her own place. I didn't know she had me in a home for pregnant girls. I didn't know all kinds of things. I never knew she was in a foster home, or that she was an orphan. How would I have known that? Who would have told me?

She had so many choices. Even after she got pregnant with me, she had choices. And still she chose Oak Grove. Apparently, she chose Dad. I clearly have no idea who my mother really was. The mother in my memories could not be the person who wrote these pages. My memory mother was dreamy and sensitive. Magical.

I want to know, did she change, or was the magic just in my imagination.

Colby and I watch two movies. One starts just before noon, and the other just before three. Both of them suck. The good ones are all rated R. I guess the girl in the ticket booth is on some kind of power trip because she won't let us buy tickets to those since I'm only fourteen. I recognize her. She goes to school with us in Oak Grove. She smiles at Colby though, right before we walk away. All sweet and giggly. I look at her close. She's pretty. She has straight blonde hair and braces. Just the fact that she has braces means she's one of those girls. The kind with married parents and sweet sixteen birthday parties.

So I think about that for the first half of the first movie, wondering if that girl has a crush on Colby. I guess that's allowed. I suppose he should have girls chasing him. But that makes me wonder why he doesn't already have a girlfriend. This is something we've never talked about. If he did get a girlfriend, where would that leave me?

We come out of the second movie, and it's almost five. By the time we get back home, and Colby checks in with Rita. It's five thirty. We settle in the camper, both of us laying back on the benches, and we wait.

Mr. Dempsey calls at six seventeen.

I only hear half the conversation. Colby telling him his mother doesn't know he called. His mother never told him anything. Nothing good or bad. That he only read a newspaper article. Colby telling him he's about to graduate and hopefully go to Texas Tech. School of Architecture. Colby saying, so I have another sister. Colby saying, yes, I have two sisters and a brother. And no, I don't have a stepdad. Colby asking, "Did you know about me?"

I close my eyes when he asks this. It crushes my heart to hear my hero, my safe haven, asking this question that is really a flood of questions. Like "How could you leave me here with her?" and "Why didn't you ever come back for me?" And I hope more than anything the answer to the question he actually spoke is no. But I can't tell because Colby just nods into the phone.

"Yes, that would be great," Colby says. "I could do it this Saturday." He keeps nodding into the phone. "Oh. I understand. Okay. Okay, well just let me know when is a good time. Okay. Yes, sir. Okay. Thank you. Goodbye."

I'm mad as hell when he closes his phone. "What? He can't meet you this Saturday? He's too busy? Seriously?"

"Jade, stop," Colby says and rubs his eyes.

I sort of get that if Colby is feeling rejected, I'm only making it worse. But I'm still mad.

"He can see me on Saturday. He just doesn't know what time."

"Oh."

We lay there for a while, not talking. And I'm thinking Colby might get another parent out of this deal after all. A smart one. With a job. I'm going to feel a little left out. Left behind.

"Are you scared?" I ask him.

"Very."

"It's kind of awesome, actually," I say. "You're a long-lost dad's daydream. It's like he won the parenting jackpot with you."

Colby scrunches up his face and stares at his phone. Then he says, "He knew."

I think hard before I answer. I start to say something, like, "It could be worse, he could be around and be a loser, like my dad." But that doesn't really help. Because what's worse? A crappy dad who didn't leave you, or a seemingly decent dad who did?

"Well then he has a lot to explain," I finally say. "You should let him try. But you shouldn't be scared."

"We'll see," he says, and pushes himself up off the bench. "I have to go home. I told my mom I'd come home before seven. She wants me to do the dishes and fold my laundry."

"You want me to go with you Saturday?" I ask him.

"I don't know," he says. "I don't think so. I mean, if it goes bad, I don't want anyone around to see it."

"It's me. Not just anyone," I say, but I know what he means. It's the same reason I don't want anyone to know about Momma's journal. I want a chance to make sense of it myself before I have to explain it to someone else. "Just let me know."

When he's gone, I pull out Momma's journal. I want to get to the end of it. I want to understand, just like Colby does.

Ruby Bell   9/6/1996

I was taking Jade on walks after school to pass the time. I was kind of looking for Rita's house and kind of hoping to run into Jimmy.

But I ended up seeing Jimmy at school. I saw his truck in the parking lot as I was walking across the drop-off line. He got out and stood by the open door, and I almost tripped over the curb when I saw a blonde-haired girl slide across the seat and get out of the truck.

She stopped and smiled up into his face. And there in the parking lot, with the morning sun shining through the cars behind them, Jimmy used his whole body to push her against the side of his truck and kiss her, long and hard on the mouth. They started to separate, then she smiled and pulled him back to her, and kissed him again.

Someone bumped into me, and I had to look away. I was standing in a river of kids that flowed around me toward the main building. The bell was about to ring. By the time I got myself out of the way and turned back, all I saw was the back of Jimmy's truck as it turned out of the parking lot and disappeared behind the gym. The girl was lost in the crowd.

I was late for class because I stood there like an idiot for a while. But Mr. Clark didn't mark me tardy, maybe because it was my first time. I couldn't hear anything he said in class. He walked by and tapped on my desk once and said, "Ms. Bell, are you with us?" I nodded but I wasn't. I spent the morning like that. Like someone knocked the air out of me.

But then I started asking myself, what difference does it make? Did I really think he would just wait for me? No. But that doesn't mean he doesn't miss me. He doesn't know I'm back in town. And that's my fault. Even if he knew I was back, he might think I don't want to see him. Maybe he thought if I wanted to see him, I would have gone to his camper, or to the park.

I felt better about everything by the time school let out. And even though I normally go straight to the Early Head Start building to get Jade, this time I waited for a while to see if he would come and pick the girl up from school, like he used to do for me.

He saw me when he pulled in. He was about to take a drag of his cigarette, but his hand stopped halfway to his mouth, and he turned his head to keep his eyes on me even as he rolled slowly past.

The girl came out of the crowd and opened the truck door. She wore a dark plaid shirt over her mini-skirt, and her short legs were stout, her calves as thick her thighs. She had to hop to get up on the seat. Before they drove away, she turned and looked at me too. I guess that's something.

Maybe I expected him to tell her she couldn't ride with him. Maybe I thought he'd come back for me. I just stood there for a little while, not really feeling anything. Not believing what just happened.

After a while, the parking lot started to clear out, and it didn't make any sense that I was still there. He wasn't coming back. And that's when I felt like crying. And I felt even worse that I left Jade at Early Head Start longer than I had to for nothing.

I took her home and cried the whole time I fed her and played with her. And after she fell asleep, I crawled into my bed and tortured myself by imagining Jimmy with that girl. How could a girl with bleached blonde hair connect with someone like Jimmy? I fell asleep trying, but I just couldn't imagine him loving her the way he loved me.

I looked for him the next morning, bracing myself for the sight of them, but he wasn't there. And then I looked for her all over school. But she wasn't in any of my classes. I had to ask Carrie who she was.

Her name is Rhonda. She's a senior. She's eighteen. So it's no wonder I don't have any classes with her. Carrie laughed at me for asking about her. She called Rhonda "the latest." And I guess this is stupid, but that made me feel better. At least they hadn't been together long. I would never tell anyone else this because they wouldn't understand, but I kind of think he was just using those girls to get over me.

Now that he knows I'm back, things will be different.

I knew it! I just knew it! He loves me. I mean he has never come out and said it, but I know he does. He had to go to some trouble to find me.

I was sound asleep. It was probably two o'clock in the morning, when I heard banging on my door. At first, I thought there was a fire or something, until I peeked out the living room window to see who it was. I saw him before he saw me. He was standing there in the porch light looking down at his feet. He was nervous, I could tell.

I rubbed under my eyes to make sure I didn't look like a mascara raccoon, then pulled open the door.

I didn't ask him about the girl. We barely spoke. He kissed me, took my hair out of my ponytail and said my name over and over as he pressed me back to my room. I barely got the front door closed and locked.

That's just the way it is with us. We don't need to talk.

After dreaming about it for so many months, I woke up in his arms for the first time this morning. And Jade met her father this morning too. I took her into the bedroom when she woke up, and we were a whole family for few minutes.

She didn't like him, and I guess I wasn't expecting that. He tried to hug her but she arched her back and grunted and tried to push out of his arms. He laughed about it, but I still think she made him feel bad, because he joked and said, "Are you sure she's mine?"

168

I guess I looked sad because he said, "I'm joking, I'm joking," over and over again after that. "She's just a baby. She'll learn who I am."

Jade just stared with her rosebud mouth open when he kissed me. I thought he was going to try to make love to me with her there in the bed. But I had to go. I had to get her to Early Head Start and get to school.

I didn't want to leave. I didn't want to give him any time to spend with that girl again. And I didn't want the landlord to see him. I don't know what kind of trouble I'll be in. Or he'll be in. But I don't want to tell him he can't come over. What if I never see him again?

He was gone when I got home from school. I guess he left without anyone seeing him because I haven't heard from the landlord yet.

Ruby Bell   9/14/1996

It's been two days since Jimmy came over. After just one night, I think I miss him more now than I ever did. But I haven't seen him at the school with that girl anymore. So that's good.

I've seen her in the hall a couple of times. She stares at me. And I think that's good too. She knows who I am. I'm the one who matters to Jimmy. She was just someone he passed the time with.

It really sucks that she's eighteen. I wish I was eighteen so bad.

Mrs. Patterson bought Jade some new clothes. She said it was time since it was about to be fall, even though fall in Texas is really just more summer. It doesn't get cold until November or December.

It's funny because even though I don't remember my mother, buying clothes for an imaginary season change it seems like something she used to do.

Mrs. Patterson asked me about getting Jade's picture made. I only have the set of pictures they took in the hospital when she was born. I have drawn dozens and dozens of pictures of her, but I never thought about getting pictures taken.

Mrs. Patterson set up an appointment at Sears, all the way over in Fairview, and came to pick us up on Saturday. I had a hard time getting the car seat strapped into the back, because Mrs. Patterson's car only has two doors. Then, I felt sick all the way to Fairview, partly because riding in cars still makes me feel like the earth is going to spiral out from under me.

Being around Mrs. Patterson is so weird. I have no idea why she's so nice to me. She says I have so much potential. I don't even know what that means. Potential for what? And how am I supposed to know how to act around her when I don't even know what it is she likes about me. But she insists. Always.

And I feel like a liar. Sometimes she'll say things about how I'm going to be a single mom, and I'll need to be able to take care of Jade. And I don't tell her I have no intention of being a single mom. And I kind of get mad that she thinks it's so easy to cut Jimmy out of Jade's life. Out of my life.

And even though I've only seen him once since I've been back, I feel like there's an entire world in my heart that I'm keeping from her.

But Jade loved Mrs. Patterson right from the start. The little stinker. My baby girl has her own mind. And it's frustrating but I'm glad. I can tell she isn't going to be scared of everything like I am. She'll have friends and join clubs and maybe even be a cheerleader. She'll have her parents to take care of her.

She got up on all fours today and rocked back and forth. She smiled so big when she did it. She'll be crawling any day now. Good thing I only have the rented furniture that came with the apartment, so there isn't anything to baby proof.

Ruby Bell _____ 9/30/1996

So now Mrs. Patterson wants to take us everywhere. She wants to take us to the park, and to the children's museum in Austin, and to some playscape thing in the mall. I guess I don't mind it. Jade's getting bigger and it's good for her to get out and see things besides our apartment and Early Head Start.

She's CRAWLING! And she has both of her bottom teeth. She looks so funny crawling around, with her mouth hanging open and drool running over those two rabbit teeth. She's such a serious baby, but she's very happy with herself now that she can go where she wants.

Jimmy came over again on a Friday. He was still there Saturday morning when Mrs. Patterson came to pick us up. Mrs. Patterson doesn't know Jimmy's truck. She didn't know he was there because he was still asleep, in the back bedroom, when she came in.

I didn't want to leave. It was our first chance to get to spend a day together as a family. But I had to go with Mrs. Patterson. I thought about telling her I was sick, or Jade was sick. But I know her. She'd try to take us to the doctor. She's just in my business all the time.

When I got home, the landlord asked me if I knew anything about that ford truck that was in the parking lot. I lied and said I didn't even notice it.

CHAPTER 13

I'm flying through these pages as fast as I can. The parts without Dad seem so clean. Untainted by his bullshit. The fact that she was independent of him is amazing to me. The parts with Dad make me sick. I know how this story ends, but still I'm willing the girl who wrote all these words to have enough common sense, to care enough about herself to want better than him.

And I'm thinking back to the time I first met Mrs. Patterson. The first time I remember meeting her, anyway. I feel like it was some kind of joke played on me. She already knew me. She knew me well. And I had no idea.

I turn the page and there, taped to a piece of sketch paper is a picture of me and my mother. It's bigger than wallet sized, but it doesn't take up the whole page. In the picture, I'm sitting on a carpeted platform and Momma's standing behind me. We're both smiling. I'm reaching up, my mouth is open just a little bit, and I'm looking at something above me.

My mother is beautiful. I remember believing she was beautiful. I'm sure everyone thinks that about their mom when they're little. So I'm surprised to look at her now and see that it was true. Her face was like a sculpture or something. Her cheeks and nose and lips so perfect. Like a doll. Her eyes are huge, clear and bluish green. She has the longest eyelashes, like I wish I had. Her hair is the same as in my memory. Red and fiery, like a lion's mane.

You always think beautiful people have everything. That doors just open, and the world will do anything for them. But maybe that isn't true if those beautiful people don't know how beautiful they are.

I stare at her face, frozen in time on this page. She looks happy. All of a sudden, I'm crying. I really thought I'd never get to see her face again.

I don't know when or if Dad will be home, so I put the binder away. What I really want is to fall asleep looking at this picture of us.

I dream about her. And in my dream, she's not happy. Everything's distorted, like a funhouse mirror. Dad is with her in this dream, even though I don't have any actual memories of them together. They're up in the bunk together, and she's crying and telling him she loves him. And she's sorry. So sorry. She's saying it's all her fault.

When I wake up, I remember how she always used to say she was sorry. It was one of the things she said most. I love you so much. And I'm so sorry. I remember how she wouldn't get up, sometimes for days. She'd cry when Uncle Ellis was gone. At least on her better days she would cry. Other days, she would just stare into space.

I take the binder with me when I go to babysit Jathan, so I can read after he goes to sleep. I cannot wait to see his face. To hear his laugh.

He opens the door when I get there and starts talking before I even get inside. He's telling me everything he got for Christmas and pulling me by the hand back to his room so I can see the new Lego Star Wars sets he already has put together.

Sheila's in the kitchen, and she comes into the living room to say hello. She watches me walk by, and she has this funny look on her face. A little ripple of fear goes through me. I don't know what's wrong. Maybe she's disgusted with me now that she knows how I live. Maybe someone told her about Dad and the people he knows. She's probably been thinking about it ever since yesterday, and probably regrets asking me to babysit. Maybe now she really is scared I'll steal something. But I don't have time to figure this out before Jathan drags me away.

Later, she calls us back to the kitchen to eat dinner. And she's super nice to me. And she keeps asking if I've gotten enough to eat. She wants to make sure I know where the towels are, and that I'm comfortable sleeping in the guest bedroom. Mr. Miller is passing dishes and smiling and nodding at me like a mental person. The whole situation is so weird. It's a relief when Mr. Miller says it's time for them to go and helps Sheila get her coat on.

Then it's just me and Jathan, and we play Clue and Trouble and Uno and watch Madagascar on their giant TV. He tells me all about the things he's been doing on his break. Ice skating and bowling and to a place full of trampolines called Jump Street with his friend Emilio. He's talking to me about everything, and I don't want him to stop so I let him fall asleep on the couch. Then I have to wake him up and make him go to bed.

I go into the guest bedroom and pull my pajamas out of my bag. I know it's a little kid thing to do, but I pretend it's my room. I pretend Jathan and I live in this house with normal parents, and we are normal rich kids with everything. I fold back the flowery bedspread and climb into the double bed. Then I reach over and find the switch for the lamp on the bed side table. A bedside table. I feel like a princess.

I pull out Momma's binder.

Rita came to pick me and Jade up on Saturday afternoon. She said Jimmy sent her. I don't really know what to say to her now. She was the closest thing I ever had to a friend here in Oak Grove. But I don't know what the situation is with her boyfriend, or her two kids. She doesn't seem like she wants to talk to me about it either. I tried to talk to ask how she was doing. I told her I'd been wondering where she lived, just trying to make some conversation.

I guess she was in a hurry to get back to her kids, because she barely even looked at Jade. She wasn't rude or mad or anything. But she didn't act like my friend, like she used to. She acted like she was on an errand for Jimmy.

We met Jimmy in the Dairy Queen parking lot where we moved Jade's car seat over to his truck. I sat in the middle of the seat and put Jade by the passenger door, as much to keep her out of Jimmy's cigarette smoke as to be next to him.

We were out on the road before I asked where we were going. I almost panicked when he said he was taking us to Ellis' house. But I kept reminding myself I'd only ever seen Ellis once. I know I'm just being ridiculous about things, like riding in cars. I manage to get through car rides without flipping out, so I know I can get through a visit to Ellis' house.

He drove us way out into the country, down winding farm to market roads, through fences and over cattle guards. Jade fell asleep, and after a few turns, I knew I wouldn't be able to find my way out there again if I had to.

Jimmy talked the whole time he drove. He told me the Hoyles were like brothers to him. He said he grew up with the Hoyle brothers, hunting on their ranch, skinny dipping in their creek, riding four wheelers and chopping cedar.

It was the most he ever told me about himself, and it helped. I could almost picture Ellis as a little kid in a creek throwing mud at Jimmy for hiding his clothes.

The Hoyles live in a big brick house, but it doesn't look like a rich person's house. It's only one story. It's huge, but the low roof makes it look ordinary.

Jimmy parked under the carport and walked into the house without even knocking. I carried Jade in her car seat so she wouldn't wake up.

Inside the house was like a cave. The front rooms were dark and paneled, and the walls were covered in cowboy paintings and animal heads. There was old, fancy furniture in the dining room. Every shelf and table we passed was covered with doilies and old things like brass clocks, and old-timey phones.

At the end of the hall was a den, a room so big that even with so much furniture, it felt empty. There were couches and tables floating out in the middle of nothing, too far away from each other. I've never seen a TV so big.

There was a bar at one end of the room, and on the other side was a flowery decorated kitchen that made me feel like there might be a mom around somewhere. On the other end of the room was a sliding glass door. Outside of it was a patio, and past that a big yard.

It wasn't Ellis on the couch, but a guy who looked like him. Only softer. More fatherly, maybe. Harmon. I knew him from the carnival. But he didn't speak. The girl sitting next to him did. She was from the carnival too. The one with the bright hair and a tattoo on her chest.

She asked Jimmy, "Who ya got with ya this time?" and right away I didn't like her. She looked me over like someone asked her what she thought of me. Then she said, "Well at least this one doesn't have her tits hangin' out. I thought I was gonna have to beat that last one down if she didn't stop flauntin' her shit around my ol' man."

She reminded me of Genesis, sort of. Too young to be so loud and pushy. She sat right next to Harmon, practically under his arm. He watched her talk with this smile on his face, like he knew she was mean, and he thought it was funny.

Jimmy didn't tell them Jade was his baby. Maybe they already knew. The girl told me to sit down, and I did. Then she started describing me to Harmon as if he couldn't see me for himself.

"Well, this one's all timid an' shit. What's with that Jimmy? I thought you liked your women loud. Like, what's that song where it goes 'I like my women a little on the trashy side!"

Harmon didn't tell her to shut up, but he told her to go get him a glass of sweet tea, and when she went into the kitchen it got quiet. That's when I learned her name, Courtney. When he talked to her.

After she was out of the room, Harmon smiled at me, just a flash of really white teeth in his suntanned face. There was no threat in him at all, just amusement, that's the best word. Like he was the smartest person in the world. Like he saw everything, and everything was a big joke.

I didn't know he was high until she sat back down beside him, and he picked up his little metal pipe. I expected Jimmy to say something or do something about Harmon smoking pot in the same room as Jade, but he didn't. No, Jimmy leaned forward, and then Harmon passed the pipe to him. He took a hit, right there next to our baby, while she was sleeping in her car seat under the haze.

Courtney was the one who noticed the look on my face, but she didn't understand. She said, "Jimmy, did you bring some kind of a narc up in here? Look at her face, like she's never seen anyone smoke a little weed before."

Jimmy finally looked at me, and I looked at Jade hoping he'd at least understand. I guess he did, but I think I made him mad. He sounded kind of huffy when he asked Harmon if I could put Jade in the back room. Harmon said, "Yeah, man, that's cool," and Jimmy picked up the car seat and took her down a different hall than the one we came in. I wanted to follow him, to see where he was putting her, but I was scared. So I asked him when he came back if I'd be able to hear her if she cried. He said yes, but I wasn't sure.

Then Courtney handed me the pipe. Harmon was watching me through his slitted eyes, and Jimmy looked at me like he just knew I was going to embarrass him in front of his friends. So I took it.

I didn't even cough. I just had the feeling that it would be bad if I did. I held it down, and let it out slowly and handed the pipe back while my lungs burned like someone had set a fire in my chest.

Then I lost myself for a while. Courtney laughed every time she looked at me, and asked Jimmy if I was okay. My mouth was so dry, and it felt like there were marbles on my eyelids holding them down. I listened to Harmon and Jimmy talk without understanding them, watching how their gestures and expressions didn't match their words at all.

Harmon talked to Jimmy like a pesky little brother. I could tell that Jimmy appreciated it and resented it at the same time. Harmon held Jimmy down with his words, teased him, kept him in his place. It was so subtle and so interesting. If I hadn't been high, I never would have seen it.

I was so into my own thoughts, I sort of forgot I was even in the room. Which is why I almost screamed when Ellis came in from the hallway carrying Jade in his arms. I wanted to jump up and take her from him, but I was moving in slow motion. I had only managed to sit up and scoot to the end of the couch cushion when I realized Jade wasn't crying. Ellis was playing with her, talking to her.

She had her tiny hand wrapped around his giant finger, and I saw the legs of her sleeper were unsnapped. He looked at me then with his electric blue eyes. I felt it again, even through my disconnected daze, a current of electricity that just paralyzed me where I was.

He said, "She was soaked, so I changed her diaper."

Courtney spoke up first. She made fun of him and called him "Ellis the Nanny." She spoke so fast, her movements so jerky, it was almost painful to me in my fluid state of mind. I looked at her harder and saw the glass pipe in her hand.

I tried to stand up. I was going to get Jade from Ellis. Somewhere in my mind ideas were trying to form. Ideas about what Ellis might have done to my baby. The idea that I had no way to leave.

But Ellis told me to sit my stoned ass down. He called Jade his little buddy, hitched her up high in the crook of his arm and took her into the kitchen. When he came back Jade was chewing on a cookie, and he had a glass of tea in his free hand. He walked right by me to the sliding glass door, and took her outside into the fresh air of the patio. I watched them in the light. I still felt like I wasn't actually there.

Harmon didn't offer me his pipe again. But Jimmy took the glass one from Courtney, and I wondered what was in it. I didn't ask. I needed to concentrate on getting my mind together, so I could figure out how to get out of there. To get my baby away from Ellis Hoyle.

It took me forever to get up the nerve to go outside and sit on the patio. The sun was sinking behind the house, and the shadows were long and interesting in a way I'd never noticed before. I was wondering how I would know when I wasn't high anymore.

Thank God Ellis didn't look at me when he first started talking to me. I don't think I could have answered if I'd met his eyes again. He was looking at Jade when he asked what I was doing there.

I said I came with Jimmy. He told me I didn't belong with Jimmy. I didn't take time to think about what he meant. I just started babbling about why I did belong with Jimmy. I was telling him things, trying to get him to understand things, and I have no idea why. I wanted him to know that I did belong with Jimmy. That Jimmy cured every fear I ever had.

He didn't answer, just looked at me like he was disappointed, like he had known me for a long time. Maybe I was smacking my lips. He handed me his glass of tea, and I didn't think about it, I just drank half of it down, I was so thirsty.

Then he stood up and took Jade out into the yard. That giant man sat on the ground with her and let her crawl over him. She wrinkled up her nose and laughed when she ran her hands over the blades of grass.

I watched them. The shadows got longer, and my thoughts became less and less interesting to me. He carried her around and showed her the leaves on the trees and held roly-poly bugs in his hand for her to see. And then he held her hand to keep her from putting them in her mouth.

The sun finally disappeared, and Ellis asked me when Jade needed to eat. He said it was after eight. It had been hours. I jumped up and started to open the door, but it was so heavy I could only get it open a few inches before it was wedged in its tracks. Ellis reached his arm around me and slid it open like it was nothing.

Inside, Harmon was asleep on the couch with one leg draped over Courtney, who was sitting there picking at her fingernails and peeking up at the TV like she was scared of it.

Jimmy was staring at the TV too, bouncing one leg up and down, like he was in a hurry to leave. When I reached for Jade's bag, he smiled in that way that used to work like magic on me when I first met him. I tried to feel like I did back then, but I just couldn't. Everything felt wrong.

I went into the kitchen to mix up Jade's bottle without asking permission. Courtney said something about me making myself at home. Ellis looked at her and her eyes got big for a second, then she went back to picking her nails, muttering, "I was just sayin', I thought she was all timid, but I guess she ain't."

I finally got Jade out of Ellis' arms and sat her on my knees to feed her. And then I held her close to me while she fell asleep and finished off her bottle. I knew she was in a deep sleep when she let go of her hold on the nipple with a tiny little sigh.

Jimmy nudged me. Then he took my hand and pulled me up off the couch. He led me toward that same hallway where he took Jade earlier.

Courtney cackled and said, "Use a towel this time Jimmy. I'm tired of cleaning up your mess."

I didn't look at her, or Jimmy. For some reason I only looked at Ellis, who watched us go with no expression on his face.

Jade's car seat was on the floor of a bedroom that looked like it was decorated for a girl. It made me wonder about the Hoyles and who lived here. I wanted to know whose room this was. Who could have decorated?

I laid Jade down in her car seat, and let Jimmy pull me onto the bed.

He moved fast, and he was rough, and it hurt, and I thought it would never end. And I thought about the first time with him, when it hurt, and I didn't care. And I thought about the last time, at my apartment when he was gentle, and he looked at me. And I thought about Ellis in the other room, and I felt like a mannequin who might not really exist at all.

Ellis ended up driving me and Jade home that night. I think Jimmy forgot about us for a while. When I started to fall asleep on the couch, Ellis offered to give us a ride. Jimmy said that was good because he didn't want the landlord to see me getting out of his truck, and that makes sense. I keep telling myself that Ellis is like a brother to Jimmy. Jimmy wouldn't have us around anyone he didn't trust.

Ellis didn't talk on the way home, and neither did I. He turned up the radio, and I guess I was surprised. I never would have thought that he listened to country music.

It's late when I finish reading this. I wish I hadn't read it. My mother high. My father using her, then leaving Uncle Ellis to take of her. I wonder why she was always so sorry? Dad deserved everything he got.

I turn off the lamp and slide down into the princess bed.

I want my mother. I pretend she's asleep down the hall. And that she's safe and happy, like she was in the picture.

When I wake up, Mr. and Mrs. Miller are home, and I try to leave right

185

away. Mr. Miller is on the couch in a pair of basketball shorts. I've never seen him in anything but slacks and a button-up shirt, and I feel like I'm invading his space.

But he doesn't seem to think it's weird at all. "Sheila's making pancakes. You hungry?"

I can't really answer because I am hungry, and I don't have a good reason to leave except that I don't belong here.

"Oh no," Sheila says coming out of the kitchen, "I made enough for you, so you have to stay and eat with us."

I stand there like an idiot, with my backpack by my feet. Then Jathan comes out of his room, and he fake kicks me on his way to the kitchen. So I put my backpack in the corner and follow him to the table. We eat pancakes, and Mr. Miller tries to be funny, and Sheila acts like the "boys" are bothering her.

I wonder about heaven. I wonder if my mother can see this.

I'm sort of worried that I should be home. I didn't tell Dad where I was going. But it's not like he was around to tell. There is the slight chance he'll come home and wonder where I am. He'll be mad if I'm gone. But since last night was New Years Eve, I bet he was busy. I bet he woke up at some girl's house. Or Uncle Ellis had to take care of him.

So I push it a little further and go with the Millers to the park when they ask. Jathan and I run around acting like little kids, swinging and sliding, hanging from monkey bars. Mr. and Mrs. Miller sit at a picnic table and watch us. The sun is out today, even though it's a little cold. I can see frost in Jathan's breath. He is laughing at me because my hair is standing straight up from going through the plastic tunnel slide.

I'm hanging upside down on the monkey bars when I see Uncle Ellis' truck. If ever I wanted to disappear, if ever I have willed myself to vanish, it's right now. He recognizes me. And he slows down. I swing my arms up and land on my feet, moving too fast, probably. Probably looking like I'm hiding something. I don't even think about it, so I guess it's instinct that makes me stand in front of Jathan, to block him from Uncle Ellis' view.

He parks his truck next to the police station and rolls down the window. I don't know what to do. Maybe I think if I talk to him, he'll leave. Or maybe it's just habit, but I walk over to his truck, knowing that Mr. and Mrs. Miller are watching me. I know they'll wonder about him. They'll wonder about me, and how I know someone like him. But I can't ignore him.

"Looks like fun," he says when I walk up. He squints in the sunlight, looking at the monkey bars.

"We're just goofing around."

"Who's that kid?"

"Just a kid I babysit," I say. Maybe a little faster than I should.

"Hmm," he says. "You like this kid?"

I slow down this time. "He's cool."

"And his parents?"

"Yeah, they're okay," I say.

"You need anything?"

"I'm good. Dad was home a few days ago."

Uncle Ellis only nods. I think we're about to be done. That he only wanted to check on me. Then Jathan comes running over.

Time slows down. I hear Jathan's feet hitting the ground behind me. It takes forever just to turn my head. I can't find any words to stop him.

"Jade! Jade! Check out what I just did!" he yells out to me. Before I can do anything he's there, and he's pulling on my arm. "I did a back flip off that top bar!"

Uncle Ellis looks at him. Locks eyes on him. Jathan freezes, like everyone does when they see Uncle Ellis' eyes. I put my arm in front of Jathan, reach across and grab his other shoulder so I can spin him around and send him back to the playground. His mouth is hanging open, just a little bit, while he stares at Uncle Ellis.

"I'll be right there," I finally manage to say. "Give me just one second." I get him turned around, and he starts back, only looking over his shoulder a couple of times as he goes.

Uncle Ellis watches him leave. "How old is he?"

"He's almost ten," I lie.

"He's big for ten," Uncle Ellis says.

"Yeah, he is."

He's squinting again, watching Jathan.

"Uh, I better get back," I finally say.

He nods, pulls his eyes off Jathan and looks at me. "You need anything, you call me."

I don't even tell him I'm fine, or that Dad can take care of me. I just say, "Yes, Sir."

I run back to the playground. I'm headed straight for the monkey bars. But Sheila calls me to the table.

"Jade, who is that man in the truck?" she asks, all chirpy, instantly back to getting on my nerves.

"He's my Uncle Ellis," I say. "He was just checking on me."

She smiles but looks worried. She watches his red truck rolling slowly away.

"He's a rancher," I say, "That's why he has that big cow pusher. I know it looks redneck."

Mr. Miller laughs, and that makes Sheila laugh. I play it off like I'm just embarrassed and run back to the monkey bars. I go back to playing with Jathan and pretend like I'm a little kid without a worry in the world. But Uncle Ellis' visit sucked all the fun out of the park. So I tell the Millers I can't stay for lunch, even though they're practically begging me to eat with them.

When I get home, I slip into the camper without telling Colby I'm back and start reading the next entry in Momma's journal. I'm reading faster now. I can't go back to school not knowing what happened.

Ruby Bell   11/7/1996

Rita still comes to pick me and Jade up. And sometimes Jimmy asks Rita to babysit Jade so I can go to parties or hang out with his friends.

His friends treat me different than the other girls hanging around at parties. They don't cuss, and they give me their seat. One time, when Jimmy came in with me, they made another girl leave. I think she must have been one of the girls he dated while I was gone. If dated is the word for it.

Sometimes, mostly when he's drunk, Jimmy talks to me about things. Probably about things he shouldn't tell me. Like how Ellis and Harmon are his only real friends, and the rest of the people he knows are just like his herd of sheep. Except for me and Jade. He says we're like royalty in his world. That he and Harmon and Ellis are the kings.

And I can see how that's true. People fall all over themselves, trying not to make Jimmy mad, trying to make him think they're cool. They want in. In on what, I'm not sure. I guess there's the money, and the business opportunity, but there's something else. They want his approval for some reason. Just like I do, I guess. And he knows it, and he uses it to get what he wants.

I don't know why he wants me. No one else ever wanted me. But he does. And because he does, they all act like I'm his queen.

He gives me money, and sometimes he takes me and Jade shopping in Fairview. My baby has new toys and nice things. I have a new TV and VCR that I keep in my bedroom so Mrs. Patterson won't ask questions when she comes over. I have everything I could ever think to want. I got my driver's license too. And I'm putting money back, hoping I can get my own car soon. For the most part, things are fine.

School is going good. Or I should say, going well. My English teacher corrected me for using good as an adverb on one of my papers. I'm trying to write better. Maybe I'll try to be a writer one day. I made all A's last six weeks, and Jimmy makes a big deal out of that. He says I'm classy in some way that none of the other girls are.

But then there are so many nights when he doesn't come by. Entire weekends pass. I spend the daylight hours with Mrs. Patterson, wishing I knew where he is and what he's doing. Then I go to sleep and wonder who he's with.

I'm not stupid, even though I pretend to be. I figured out what was in the glass pipe. I see what it's doing to his body, to his teeth, to his skin. I know how he gets when he's on it. I know what he likes to do.

He keeps telling me it's okay. That he's going to quit. That he can be in the business and not let the life get him. Harmon and Ellis don't use at all, he says. But I know why they don't. Harmon and Ellis don't "work the herd." That's what Jimmy calls it. He has to be around the people who do it. Harmon and Ellis don't. The temptation is always there for Jimmy, and it's just too much for him.

Ruby Bell   12/2/1996

Jade and I spent Thanksgiving at Mrs. Patterson's house. Her husband died a few years ago, and her two sons live in Boston or someplace like that. Maybe Baltimore, I can't remember. I know it made her so happy to have us there, but it felt so wrong. Jimmy keeps promising he's going to take me to meet his mother and the rest of his family, his mom and brother. I asked Rita about it, and she said she doesn't know why I even want to meet them, that I'm not missing much.

But they're Jade's family. It's her first Thanksgiving. And the only memory we will have is of us spending it with a practical stranger. And honestly, the person Mrs. Patterson thinks I am, the person she thinks she knows, doesn't exist.

Then to make matters worse, after Mrs. Patterson took us home on Thanksgiving, some guy named Oliver came by my apartment. It was probably ten o'clock that night, and he told me Jimmy was at a party, and he couldn't drive home. I kept asking why he couldn't drive. Oliver didn't want to tell me, but finally he said Jimmy had shot heroine.

Jade was already asleep. I wasn't about to take her with me. I didn't even know where the party was, but I knew she didn't need to go. So I left her sleeping in her crib and rode with Oliver back to the party.

I didn't recognize the house. I asked Oliver whose house it was, and he said it was Rhonda's. Or her mom's. I can't believe anyone could live in a place like that. There was handwriting and spray paint on the walls, at least in the places where the sheetrock wasn't torn away. I could see insulation and electric wiring between the wooden boards inside the wall behind the couch.

Jimmy was on the end of the couch, and Rhonda was there beside him, crying mascara streaks down her pudgy face. She looked at me like I was there to save her.

"He won't wake up. Ruby, I'm so sorry. I am so sorry," she kept saying over and over again, like we were friends, like we had ever met before. I'm such an idiot, I told her it was okay. But it wasn't. And I didn't know what to do.

Oliver offered to help me carry him out to his truck, and we managed to get him into the passenger seat. Then I crawled up into the driver's side.

I took him back to my apartment. I didn't know where else to go. Then, it took forever, but I finally got him to wake up enough to make it inside. He flopped down on my couch and laid there, panting so hard, I started getting scared he was going to die.

So I called Ellis.

If it hadn't been Thanksgiving, I don't know if he would have been home. He answered on the third ring. I could tell he was mad, he was so short with me. I told him I wouldn't have called except I thought Jimmy was going to die. I told him I was sorry, and that seemed to make him even more mad.

"Why are *you* sorry?" he asked, then hung up on me.

It was almost half an hour later when he knocked on my door. I pulled it open and sort of panicked when I saw him, he looked so mad. I always forget how big he is, how ruthless his eyes are.

He barely looked at me, and I felt like such an idiot, needing his help.

"He's on the couch," I told him. Then when he looked me over again, I realized I was blocking the door, and he was waiting for me to move.

I told him Oliver said I should put him in a cold bath to get him to snap out of it, but he was too heavy to get down the hall. And Ellis said, "Lucky for Jimmy you're so small. That probably would have killed him." He moved past me and got down in front of the couch to look at Jimmy.

I stood behind him and he pulled a bag of orange capped needles out of his pocket. Then he had a tiny glass bottle in the palm of his hand.

That scared me enough that I asked him what he was doing, and he said he was going to give Jimmy Narcan. I asked what Narcan was, and he asked if I wanted a chemistry lesson, or if I wanted him to save Jimmy.

So I closed my mouth and watched him slip the needle into Jimmy's arm. It occurred to me right then, while Jimmy's struggling heart moved that blue fluid through those thin veins, how very delicate life is. What a fine and complicated balance. How easily lost.

I backed up until I felt the chair behind my legs, then I let myself fall into it. I had to press my hand to my mouth to keep from throwing up. When he was done, Ellis sat back on his heels, put the little bottle and needle down, and loosened the tubing. Then he turned around and asked me how Oliver knew where I lived, and what in the hell he was doing coming to my house.

I told him I guessed Jimmy sent him. Or Rhonda.

"He was with Rhonda?" he asked me "And she sent that piece of shit over here to your house?" I didn't know how to answer him. I knew there were unspoken rules about me. I just didn't know they were Ellis' rules.

Jimmy coughed and threw up on the couch cushion, and I ran to the kitchen to get a wet towel. When I came back he was awake, and I cleaned him up and helped him get his shirt off. Even though I was mad at him, I was more relieved.

Ellis didn't help me at all. He sat down in the chair I just left and watched me. Glowered. Maybe that would be a better word.

Once I got the couch cleaned up, I went down the hall and drained the cold bath water then started the shower. I tried to help Jimmy to the shower by myself, but he almost crushed me when he put his weight on me. Ellis must have gotten tired of watching us struggle after a few tries, because he finally got up to help

Then Jimmy was under the running water, warm this time, and Ellis and I were there in the tiny bathroom together. I forced myself to look at him, to try to see him as the kid Jimmy described.

Then I said it to him, "Jimmy told me about how you guys used to play together when you were kids." It was such a random thing to say.

He didn't soften one bit that I could see. He didn't answer me. He just reached out and picked up one of my curls, his hand brushing my collar bone, then he laid it back down just as gently and walked out of the bathroom. He was gone when I went to get a towel for Jimmy from the hall closet.

I helped Jimmy to my bed by myself. He cried in my arms and told me he loved me for the first time. He made me promise I'd never leave him. That's all it took. I forgot all about Rhonda and Ellis and everything.

CHAPTER 14

Ruby Bell 1/6/1997

Christmas break was amazing. Jimmy was finally feeling better after his OD but still feeling guilty about the whole Rhonda thing. I guess Ellis gave him a hard time about letting Oliver come to my house. A hard enough time that Jimmy had a black eye and sore ribs after their talk. According to Jimmy, Ellis has a very strong "don't shit where you eat policy." But he promised me it was all cool with him and Ellis because they were like brothers, and sometimes brothers fight.

Jimmy had Rita drop him off at my house, and he stayed in the apartment with me for days on end. We spent those days just being together, being a family. Jade says "Dad" now. And on Christmas Eve, she fell asleep in Jimmy's arms while he watched TV.

He stayed still long enough for me to sketch them, even though I could have done it from memory. Her hair is dark and straight like his, but she has my mouth and eyes. And who can tell about her tiny nose, and round cheeks. Those look the same on all babies if you ask me.

Jimmy says my drawings are bad ass, and he doesn't understand why I won't let anyone else see them. And he calls me babe. I love that.

He helped Jade open her presents, and I made bacon and eggs for breakfast. And we napped and watched TV and played with Jade's toys. It was perfect.

The sketch is on the next page. Me and Dad and a Christmas tree. It's a little nauseating how easily she made him look like some kind of loving father. He was nothing but a junkie. I don't know what would make him keep coming back around Momma, when she was so obviously not his kind. Except she was beautiful. But she was an idiot for thinking he ever cared. An absolute idiot.

<u>Ruby Bell</u>   <u>2/10/1997</u>

Jade had two birthday parties, one with me and Mrs. Patterson, who took us to the inflatable playscape in the mall. Then we got an ice cream cake at Baskin Robins. I was really grateful to Mrs. Patterson for that. I'm starting to realize that she wants things for me and Jade that we won't ever get to have with Jimmy.

Jade's other birthday party was at the Hoyles' house. Courtney and I put out the cake and ice cream and Ellis showed her the plastic playhouse and car he bought her so she'll have something to play with when we're at their house. Harmon bought her a pair of baby Nikes and a Ralph Lauren outfit that probably cost more than a hundred dollars. I have to make sure Mrs. Patterson never sees those.

Rita brought her kids to the Hoyles' house. Colby's almost four, and he's the most tender-hearted little boy I've ever seen. Every time I see him, I want to pull him up into my lap and hug him, but he doesn't trust me yet. I don't think I've ever seen Rita show him any affection, and it breaks my heart. I might think Rita doesn't know how to be nice to her kids at all, but she plays with the little girl all the time. The little girl, Shelby, is sweet too I guess, but I don't know why Rita favors her so much.

Courtney says Rita doesn't like either of her kids, she's just good to Shelby because her daddy is a meal ticket. Courtney talks too much. She has an opinion about everything.

I did manage to get a smile out of Colby once. I put icing on my nose and crossed my eyes when I handed him his cake. And he laughed for a second, before he caught himself. Ellis took all the little ones outside, bundled up in coats so thick their arms stuck out. I watched them out there playing with Ellis, and I was jealous of their fearlessness.

If someone walked in right then and didn't know us, they might think it was a real family birthday party. Except Jimmy got stoned and fell asleep on the couch. I guess I shouldn't have forced the birthday party on him. He was right that she wouldn't remember it. And he was right that we didn't have anywhere but the Hoyles' house to have a party. And he was right, we aren't those kind of parents.

But I want to be those kind of parents.

Ellis drove me home again. We didn't talk. We never do. I sang Barney songs to Jade until she fell asleep. And then there was silence. Silence enough for me to think about why Ellis is always the one to drive me home.

Ellis carried Jade's car seat to the door. The landlord's light was off, and Jade is really getting heavy, so I let him carry her in. He set her on the couch in the dark living room.

He stopped on his way out the door, the size of him almost blocked out the light from the street. I thought he was going to say something, the way he turned his head back and looked at me. I tried to think of what animal he reminded me of. Like a cat of some kind.

I guess wanting to know what he thinks of me is starting to outweigh being scared of him.

Ruby Bell   2/19/1997

Carrie was the one who finally told me. All this time, everyone knew except me. I knew he cheated on me, but I didn't understand. Not really.

The real deal is that when Rhonda doesn't have money for drugs, Jimmy gives them to her for sleeping with him. Or whatever else he might want her to do. And she isn't the only one. She's just one of them. Carrie called her a strawberry.

It doesn't make sense. How can I love him so much if he doesn't care for me any more than that? Honestly, I can't deal with this. I just can't handle it. I feel like my whole life is just too much. It's just unreal. And it hurts.

Ruby Bell _____ 2/28/1997

I go to school, and it's like another world. Like a parallel universe. I see all these girls who are my age, and we sit in the same classes and do the same homework. But they live with their parents and get grounded if they come home too late. They gripe if their mother makes them clean their room or do their own laundry. I listen to them talking about going bowling and to the movies, and I cannot imagine what that would be like.

But there is this guy at school, and he keeps following me around. He knows I have a baby, which makes me wonder why he can't get a normal girl without all the baggage. He has friends. He plays sports, runs track, I think. He seems normal.

And then Carrie tells me these things about Jimmy, and for a little while I can't really remember that feeling I had for him. And he hasn't come over or sent anyone to get me since I asked him about Rhonda.

I thought we would have a huge fight about Rhonda. I thought I would tell him how I feel, and he would have the decency to apologize, or tell me he would never see her again. But he just threw up his hands, said he didn't have to listen to my shit and left.

And Jade hasn't asked for him not one time. Which makes me realize that he hasn't really been around her that much anyway.

So this guy at school asked me, for the millionth time, if I wanted to go to a movie. For this I can ask Mrs. Patterson to babysit, because she'll just be so happy I'm doing a normal kid thing. I mean, she has no idea I've been seeing Jimmy since I've been back. But I know she's been worried about it, the way she asks about Rita and always makes such a production about me being a single mom.

So fine. I'm going on a date with this guy. His name is Michael.

Ruby Bell   3/3/1997

I don't know why people date. That was the most uncomfortable and awkward experience I have ever had. Michael was nice enough, but I don't ever want to do that again. It was boring, and we didn't have anything to talk about, and I couldn't wait for it to be over so I could go home to Jade.

Ruby Bell   3/8/1997

Michael asked me out again, and I said yes like an idiot. And then I regretted it for the rest of the day, even though Mrs. Patterson was so excited when I told her. She said he's a good boy and comes from a good family. Which makes me wonder what people say about me and the kind of family I come from, which is none. What will his good family think when they meet me, and Jade? I mean this is just going to be bad all the way around.

And really, what do I have in common with this guy who still lives with his mommy and daddy? I know it's not his fault, and I'm almost a year younger than him, but he is so spoiled. Or clueless. Such a kid.

But when he asked, I just said "sure", like I didn't know any other words in the English language.

Then I walked into my science class, and I heard this girl talking about Michael, and she got quieter when I came in. But she kept talking, almost whispering, and when I looked over, I saw her cutting her eyes at me.

The whole thing was about Michael's ex-girlfriend wanting to know why he would ask me out when I'm such a freak, and I hang out with those stoner kids. Or something to that effect. Anyway. The answer to the big question came from one of the guys in their group when he said, "Well, duh, why do you think anyone would ask her out? She's hot, and you know she puts out."

So, when I got home, I called Michael, and told him Jade was sick, and I couldn't go out. And then I hoped I hadn't jinxed my baby with my lying.

Ruby Bell _____ 3/17/1997

Since Jimmy got mad at me, I'm back to making my money stretch. Jade's growing so fast, I can't keep her in shoes that fit. I took her to Early Head Start in socks yesterday, rather than cramming her feet into those Baby Nikes Harmon bought her.

There's a clothes closet at the child protective services office, but it's so picked over there's never anything worth taking. So I've been babysitting for Rita to make a little extra money. She only needs a babysitter once every couple of weeks or so, when her boyfriend takes her out.

Her boyfriend's name is Clay, and he seems like a nice enough guy, but she says he's a control freak. He won't let her go to parties, and he wants his house cleaned just perfectly, and dinner on the table when he gets home.

But he bought her a car, and they live in a nice house. And her kids have what they need, so I don't think I would complain much. He seems like he's good to Colby, so that's something. I'd say he's even better to Colby than Rita is.

For me, the extra money every once in a while helps. Getting Shelby's hand-me-downs for Jade is nice too. And I like having other kids for Jade to play with.

Rita says she hasn't heard from Jimmy either. She says he only talks to her when he wants something. I don't know if I miss Jimmy, or if I'm just lonely. I keep telling myself he wasn't much company. But he was. He made me feel special, and I miss that.

I almost can't believe what I'm reading. Did my mother really come that close to giving up on Dad? I feel like cheering for her, like a character in a book or something. I want to tell her to hold out for something better. I want to send a message back in time to tell her she can find someone who'll love her the way she deserves. But I know how this ends.

Then I hate Dad all over again for being such a loser, for not appreciating her and loving her and making her feel safe. That's how he got her in the first place. He made her think he would keep her safe. That was such a dirty lie.

And it's really not hard to see why she felt so hopeless. I guess if there was a girl with a baby at school now, no one would want to date her. I feel horrible for being the reason people treated my mother like that. I was the reason she thought no one else would want her.

Then I think about Rita. Rita managed to find Shelby's dad after she had Colby, and then the twins' dad after that. If Rita can…

How could Momma not know what she was worth?

<u>Ruby Bell</u>   <u>3/31/1997</u>

I asked Rita to babysit for me and told the landlord I was spending the night at her house. Then I went to a party with Carrie. I knew Jimmy would be there, so Carrie and I caked on our eyeliner and ratted our bangs and used almost a whole can of Aqua Net.

When I looked in the mirror before we left, all I could see was me, not hidden very well under a layer of tacky wrong colored makeup and frizzy hair. Carrie said no one was going to notice my base line in the headlights at a pasture party. But I know they noticed the miniskirt I borrowed from Carrie, and the push-up bra too.

Every guy there was staring at me. Every time Carrie stopped to flirt with someone, they might put their arm around her and talk to her, but it was me they were checking out. I guess that sounds conceited. But that's not the point. The point is when I finally heard his voice, when I finally got myself in his sight, Jimmy was the only one who looked right through me like I didn't even exist. So, I ended up getting stoned and drinking too much. I'm sure everyone knew I was just trying to make Jimmy jealous. And it's funny how easy it is to flirt with guys when you're just putting on a show.

After a while, I figured out Jimmy was gone. Someone said he left with some other girl, Sherry, or something like that. So I was all messed up with no reason to even be at the stupid party. And this guy, I don't even know his name, but he started pulling me to him, trying to get me away from the group, trying to get his hands under my skirt. I honestly didn't care.

I didn't know Ellis was at the party. But it's just like him to be the only one sober, the only one paying attention to what's going on. It's creepy really.

I don't know how I would have felt about myself the next day if Ellis hadn't stopped that guy. I still don't know the guy's name. But at that exact moment, I was so high I was almost asleep, and everything felt pointless without Jimmy. So I didn't mind letting him do what he wanted to me nearly as much as I minded Ellis grabbing me by the arm and dragging me back to his truck.

I felt like I was outside of myself, in some dark kaleidoscope of images. I can still see the look on the guy's face as Ellis dragged me off. Irritated, then terrified of Ellis, then relieved to see me go. People stopped talking and turned to stare as we passed. The light in the cab of his truck blinded me for a second and went dark again. And I started to cry.

I woke up in my own bed. I don't really remember how I got there. The sun was beating through the window, and Rita was banging on the door. When I opened it, she handed Jade to me and said she had to go. Clay was waiting for her. I was still wearing the miniskirt and bra and smeared makeup.

Ruby Bell   4/21/1997

I guess I've been partying a lot lately. Rita says she can't keep babysitting for me, that Clay's getting tired of it. And I want to stop, but then there's Jimmy.

I saw him at a party again, and he talked to me. I wasn't going to drink or do anything, not after what happened last time. I wasn't even really expecting to see him that night. But he was there, and he was being nice to me. He passed me a joint and watched me take a hit. And then he kept making me smoke more and more, just pushing me until I choked and told him I couldn't take anymore.

And then he smiled at me and took my hand and led me into a back bedroom. He closed the door and locked it, and when he turned around, I didn't even see the look on his face before he pushed me down over the end of bed. He held me down by my hair, pushing the side of my face into the mattress. I know it seems crazy that I'm the one who undid my pants.

It felt horrible in so many ways. But it was better than being ignored. When he was done, he left me there in the room, pulling up my pants and straightening out my hair. It looked like someone's parents' room, and I smoothed out the indention my face made in the covers. Then I went out into the hall and found a bathroom so I could clean up.

When I came out, I saw Jimmy at the kitchen table, playing some kind of card game. I stood by him, and he didn't even look up at me for a while. When he did, he asked, "What do you want? You ready for some more?" He laughed at me, and the guys at the table laughed with him. Then they went back to playing cards.

It took me a second to understand. It was like I disappeared, like they all forgot I was a real person. Except for one guy who didn't look away at first. He looked like he felt sorry for me, which was how I finally understood. Then Jimmy yelled, "Jeremy! You in?" and then Jeremy looked away from me too.

I waited outside on the porch for Carrie to be ready to go, still so stoned that time could have been flying by or standing still, I wouldn't know. That's where I was when Jimmy came out. He was leaving with that Sherry girl. He stopped at the bottom of the porch steps and told her to go ahead and wait for him by his truck.

When she was gone, he pointed at me and looked so mean, like a crazy person. And he said he knew about me dating that kid from school, and he knew what I was doing with that guy at the party, and if I wanted to act like a whore, he was going to treat me like one.

And I told him I didn't do anything with either of those guys. And I begged him not to leave with that girl. And I told him I loved him, and I was sorry, and I would do anything for us to go back to the way we used to be. Like we were at Christmas.

He left with her anyway.

But he came over the next night, and he was being nice to me again. I made up my mind I would never say another word to him again about other girls, or anything, even tweaking. After that, I just tried to be with him as much as possible and do the things he likes to do with those girls, so maybe he wouldn't want them anymore.

But things aren't really getting better between us, and I can't keep leaving Jade with Rita.

❖ ❖ ❖

Now I hate Dad so bad it's festering in me. And when he comes home again on Friday, he pulls up in a car I've never seen before. He comes in, and he's slamming things around, and I just sit there glaring at him. He finally stops what he's doing and looks at me.

"What's your fucking problem?" he asks.

I don't answer him right away. But I want to. I'm going to. I want to know how he could treat my mother like she was nothing. I want to know how he thought he was ever worthy of her. How he could lure her into thinking he would keep her safe, then leave her to this life.

He's back to digging around in the refrigerator, and I keep watching him. It's coming.

"Did you know Momma kept a journal?"

The shuffling noises behind the fridge door stop. He stands up. "Yeah," he says, "I knew."

"Did you know she wrote about you? About how much she loved you?"

"She never let anyone read that thing."

"I have it."

He closes the refrigerator door. I watch him, waiting for him to look at me. I think he'll say it's full of lies. But he doesn't. He turns around and leans against the fridge with his arms crossed over his chest. Like he's thinking about something. Remembering something that doesn't have anything to do with what I'm saying.

"I'd like to see it," he says, and that surprises me.

"I bet you won't like what's in it," I say. I want to fight with him. I want him to get mad or tell me she was crazy. Something. I'm ready for a battle.

"I bet you're right," he says. Again, this is not what I expected. This is not my Dad.

"Did you ever give a shit about her?" I ask, still trying to stir up some kind of fight.

He looks at me like I've lost my mind. "Is that what she wrote? That I never cared about her?"

"Oh God no," I laugh. "No. Apparently, my poor deluded mother didn't, not for a minute, let herself think that. But it doesn't take a rocket scientist to read between the lines."

He closes his eyes and leans his head back, like he is stretching out some kind of tension in his neck or saying a prayer.

"I want to…" he starts, and then he looks like he forgot what he was going to say. "I don't…" And then he looks mad again. "Look, don't you think I miss her too?"

"Why would I think that? What have you ever done that would make me think that? You don't even talk about her." I'm yelling at him, and I'm too mad to be scared. "You know what? No, I don't think you miss her too. I can't tell if you even notice she's gone."

"I can't handle this shit," he says, and he's turning toward the door.

"You never deserved her!" I scream, like I'm trying to get this hate out of me while he's still here to take it.

He stops. "I know that," he says over his shoulder. "It doesn't take a rocket scientist to figure that out."

He opens the door. He's leaving, and I'm not satisfied.

"And you drug her into this hell hole! And then you left her here! You left her alone!"

He slams the door behind him.

Ruby Bell   5/25/1998

I haven't written in my journal in a long time because I thought there wasn't much to write about. Or maybe it was so bad, I couldn't write it down.

But I just pulled it out and read back through those last pages, and it makes me sick. So much has changed. I'm almost eighteen, and if I can take a couple of summer school classes, I can graduate at Christmas. Only a semester late, which is amazing after being out of school for so long having Jade.

I finally quit trying to fit into Jimmy's world. I picked Jade over him. That's what it came down to, really. I mean, I didn't make a stand or anything. That would never have made a difference to Jimmy, anyway. It only made things worse.

I started thinking about it once I could see the end of high school coming. I was working on my schedule for next year, and Mrs. Patterson signed me up for this new graphic art class where they use computers to draw things. We were talking about what I wanted to do after high school, like college and a job and all that. And then I entered a competition in my art class and won a prize. I was in the paper for that. They put my sketch of Jade on display in the state capital.

Jimmy felt like a huge waste of time. Everything that was so cool about him started getting really annoying. It was the same thing over and over again. The same people, the same parties. He looked like a skeleton and said he felt like crap most of the time. I still love him, but not in the same way. I'm not in awe of him like I was. Not desperate. Maybe that's part of growing up.

I think he knew I was changing just by the look on my face, or the questions I'd ask about his plan for the future, which was just to keep doing what he was doing. One time, I asked him how he'd feel if Jade ended up at one of his parties.

I mean, everyone else is growing up and getting a job, or going to prison or dying in car accidents and overdoses. The people left for him to hang out with are just getting younger and younger. So eventually, it could be our daughter, right?

I was just asking, not even trying to make a point. I quit caring so much about making him happy. I quit being impressed by his bullshit. And I quit trying to get him to care about us. I guess that wasn't any fun to him, so he quit coming around.

Then he had his big change of heart. I hadn't seen him in a really long time. Months. I wasn't dating. I quit asking people about him. I was really over him. Getting on with my life.

I was so irritated when he showed up on my porch. Irritated that I could get in trouble for having him over, and because I had to be at school the next day. I was sad, but mostly annoyed that he was still trying to use my love for him to get what he wanted.

He was sober. That was new. And he wasn't only talking about staying clean like Ellis, like before. He was talking about getting out of the business. Starting a new life. Getting a regular job. Getting married.

And he has been clean since that night. He makes it look easy. That's how I know he's serious this time. But getting out is going to be harder than staying clean, because of Ellis and Harmon. And because of his pride. I can't see him working for anyone. He likes easy money.

But he says he has a plan of some kind. I don't ask about it. The less I know, the better. He says once he does this thing, we'll be able to leave, buy a house, pay for college, whatever we want.

So we're getting married the day after my eighteenth birthday. I don't want our anniversary on my birthday. I want our anniversary to be special. It'll be a June wedding, at the justice of the peace.

I thought that was worth writing about.

Mrs. Patterson was trying to make plans for my birthday, when I told her I was getting married. She wanted to go to a ballet or a musical or something in Austin, and then maybe to an art gallery. And that sounded like something I'd really like to do, the art gallery part, because I've heard about all the cool art communities in Austin.

And I think once Jimmy comes through on his big plan, that maybe we can live downtown in a big city, and I can be a famous artist.

Mrs. Patterson quit talking when I told her I was getting married the next day. We were in her office. She was stirring her coffee, and her spoon stopped. But she didn't look up at me right away.

And so I started yammering, trying to fill the gap. I told her that Jade needed her father, and that Jimmy was clean and sober. And I told her we were going to make a new start, and he was going to pay for my college, so she could quit worrying so much about my scholarships and federal aid applications. I laughed a little there, hoping she would think it was funny. But when she looked up at me the only color in her face was the red in her eyes.

She wanted to know how long I'd been seeing him, and how long I'd been planning to get married, and if I really thought he was a good example for Jade. And didn't I think Jade deserved better.

And I told her about how I tried to date Michael, and what those other kids said about me. And how I had to face the fact that no one else was going to really love a girl with a kid. And no one else was going to love Jade like Jimmy does.

She put her head in her hands and started crying. Not just teary eyed, but she sobbed and begged me not to do it. AShe shook her head at the same time, because she had to know I already made up my mind.

I told her she would see that it was the right thing to do. She would see how different Jimmy is now. I told her she should go out to dinner with us sometime, and she would see. Except I knew Jimmy would never go out to dinner with her. Even for our wedding day, he'd never put up with that.

She said, "Just go, Ruby. I can't take anymore. Just go."

So I got up and went out into the hall, and I don't know why I was crying, but I was.

But now she knows. And in a couple of weeks, school will be out, I will be eighteen, and Mrs. Jimmy Jennings.

Ruby Jennings   6/25/1998

We moved into the camper today. We already had most of our stuff out of the apartment anyway. Now that I'm married, I don't qualify for any of those programs anymore, so I had to be out by the end of the month.

The trip to the justice of the peace wasn't much. It was a lot like a trip to the AFDC office, filling out papers and waiting our turn. Jimmy says we can have a real wedding later. But he wants me to know he's serious about us this time, so he wants it to be official.

The camper is really small. There isn't any place for Jade to play, and she gets into everything. Jimmy isn't used to having her around all the time, and I think she stresses him out. And he smokes inside, so I try to keep her outside as much as I can.

It isn't too hot yet. I decided to start a garden, just for something to do. Hopefully, I won't be around much longer. Jimmy is working on something, meeting with people. He spends a lot of time out at the Hoyles' place, but he doesn't even ask me if I want to go.

He's still clean, putting on weight, getting enough sleep. I trust him this time. He's going to get us out of here.

Ruby Jennings   7/7/1998

I stopped by Mrs. Patterson's office again today after my morning summer school class. I wanted her to know that I'm still serious about school. She let me come in and sit down, and she was nice to me. I showed her my ring, just a plain gold band, and she smiled. But it wasn't the same.

So I found myself telling her all the reasons she didn't need to worry. I told her he was different. I knew he did bad things. He did bad things to me. Things I would never tell anyone about. And I knew how he got his money. I'm not stupid.

And that's how I know things are going to be different now. I told her he was working on a plan so we wouldn't have to worry about money again.

She listened to me, but she looked like she was in some kind of horrible pain. Maybe because she didn't know about all the things I did, all while she thought she knew everything about me. And she was just finding out what a liar I am at the same time she was finding out about me and Jimmy.

So I quit talking about what already happened and tried to tell her about what Jimmy had planned. And I told her how we were going to go live in the city, which I wasn't really sure about, since Jimmy said he'd rather have a place out in the country like the Hoyles do. But I knew she would be happier if she thought I was doing something with my art.

I told her he was going to do something big so that he would have the money to pay for my college and support us, and it was going to be fine. And she didn't ask me, but I told her the camper was only temporary because Jimmy had a plan.

When I stopped talking and waited for her to say something, she just said, "I hope so Ruby. For you and for Jade, I really hope so." And she looked at me with no expression, and it took a second before I remembered that's how teachers let you know you aren't welcome anymore, that you're dismissed.

CHAPTER 15

Ruby Jennings   7/16/1998

Now I understand why it wasn't Ellis or Harmon that came to tell me what happened. Janine wouldn't let them come onto her property, she was so mad. But at first, hearing it from Rita seemed like a cruel joke. She acted like she was mad at me because Jimmy got arrested.

He was gone for so long, I started imagining all kinds of things. He didn't tell me where he was going. I never heard him making any plans. He just said it was time to get the deed done and when he got back, we'd be free to do whatever we wanted.

I didn't even ask what he meant. I trusted him. It was so easy to trust him after he was clean for so long. I mean, he always came back when he said he'd come back. He'd blow his friends off too, just to hang out with me and Jade. And he was getting more and more patient with her.

I keep thinking about that time we were all in the hammock together, and Jade fell asleep between us. And he rubbed his thumb along the arch of her eyebrow, and I knew he was thinking how beautiful she is. And he just talked and talked about what our life was going to be like, and how she would never want for anything.

All I really had were those words to bet on. None of his words ever really amounted to much before. But I still believed him.

They won't let him come home. They're afraid he'll run. And I'm sitting here alone, with my baby, feeling like we just got yanked out of our dream life and dumped here in this crackerjack box of a camper. Like it's the first time I've really noticed how bad it is. And I keep wondering how it can feel like they took something away that I never had to begin with. All I ever had were words.

Jimmy's mom had a fit when the DEA came to search the camper and her property. She acted like it was my fault, asking me what they were doing, what they wanted, if they were done yet. I know she was just taking it out on me because she wouldn't dare say those things to the agents. I'd like to think Janine is upset about what's happening to her son, what it means for his future, but I can't tell. Mostly she seems disgusted and irritated by the whole thing.

I haven't cried yet. Maybe it just doesn't seem real. Maybe it will turn out to be a mistake, and he'll be home soon.

Those agents might as well have been robots, calling me Ma'am and Mrs. Jennings. They didn't find anything in our camper. I made sure it was clean when I moved Jade in. There were things out by the fire-pit they hauled off, but I didn't see what it was. I don't think it amounted to anything useful for them. Whatever Jimmy did, he didn't do anywhere near his home. He learned that from Ellis and Harmon.

I don't want to stop reading. This is the point where my own memories start. All of those foggy reasons for what happened later are just waiting to be read.

But Colby is back from his first visit with his dad, and he wants to talk.

We're out by the burn pit because it's nice outside. He sits in one of the lawn chairs, but he can't stay still. So in a few minutes he's up and pacing.

"I look just like him," he says. "My hands are just like his." He holds them out, as if I've never seen them before.

I'm just listening. He's on a high, saying his whole life makes sense now.

"He lines his silverware up just like I do. And his cup. He didn't even think about it when he adjusted everything on the table," Colby says.

I'm thinking about all the times Aunt Rita made fun of Colby or called him weird for that. Called him OCD. Said he was going to need medicine or he'd end up like Rain Man. I wonder how things would've been for Colby if he'd grown up with a parent just like him.

I know some things probably make more sense to Colby now. The nature vs. nurture thing is going to be interesting for a while. But there are still big things that Colby hasn't talked about yet. I'm waiting for him to get to those.

"He drives a BMW," Colby says, and this seems to take the excitement out of him. He chews on the side of his lip and then sits back down, like he's trying to figure something out. "I didn't ask him why he never wanted to see me."

"What? Why?" I'm amazed. The biggest question, the first thing I think I'd demand to know, and Colby didn't even ask.

"Because he's a stranger, Jade," he says. "I felt like it would be rude."

"He's your father," I say. "He owes you an explanation."

"So I was thinking about that. If he had offered some explanation, like, I don't know, anything. Like your mom threatened me with jail, or anything, I would have been good," he says. "But he wasn't offering an explanation. So that makes me think the truth is something I don't want to hear, and that's why he isn't saying it. Maybe it's because he didn't care. And do I really need him to say that?"

I feel like someone hit me in the stomach. I don't want this to be true. I don't want Colby to believe his father knew about him and just didn't want anything to do with him. "Does he act like he cares? Does he want to see you again?" I ask.

"Yeah, he says he does," I know Colby is resetting himself. Trying to shake off his feelings and be logical again. "He says we have a lot to talk about. I don't know what that means."

"I think it means he wants to explain," I say, and Colby sinks back into the chair. He nods, like yes, that makes perfect sense. And then he lets out a deep breath, like you do when you know everything is going to be okay.

I can't help but think of Rita, in her house, less than fifty feet away, doing nothing but watching TV. No appointment necessary. It's funny that Colby never wanted her to explain.

Right at that moment, I decide. I want Dad to answer the question.

Ruby Jennings   7/23/1998

I've been to see Jimmy a couple of times. That's when I finally cried. He doesn't look anything like himself. It's the same shell. The same person that everyone always sees. But there's no fight in him, no strut, no light. He tells me he's sorry he let us all down. And not because he shouldn't have tried that deal. But because he should have known it was a setup. And he should have gotten out sooner. And he shouldn't have gotten caught.

I can picture Mrs. Patterson's face as he talks. I can feel her disapproval. I know in her world, Jimmy is sorry for the wrong thing. But I also know that in her world, life isn't a constant struggle to get by. So how would she understand why Jimmy wanted to do something drastic to get us out of the muck?

I understand it. I love him for it. I keep telling him we're going to get through it. We'll figure it out. But it looks like it's going to be a very long time. And it looks like I'm the one who's going to have to figure it out by myself.

Ruby Jennings   8/1/1998

The fall semester starts up in a couple of weeks. I don't know what I'll do about Early Head Start. I don't know if I qualify anymore, now that I'm eighteen and married. I want to go find out but keep getting stuck on my address. I don't know how I'll put the camper down as an address on the application form. I can't really focus on anything long enough to figure out what to do.

I saw Ellis today after I visited Jimmy. He was coming in as I was going out. He stopped and watched me walk by. I didn't tell him visiting hours were over. I didn't talk to him at all. I just nodded to him and pushed through the door out into the heat. I was almost to the dirt road when I heard his truck come up behind me. I stopped walking and waited, holding Jade on my hip as he slowed down beside me and rolled down the window.

He asked if we were okay. I realized I hadn't seen him in weeks. I saw his hand on the steering wheel, the size of his arm, the tribal tattoo that trailed out from under his t-shirt sleeve. Jade saw him and reached out her arms, like she couldn't feel the cold current going through me, even when I held her tighter.

I told him we were fine and didn't say anything else. He looked me over like livestock, judging me, deciding for himself if we're really okay.

He said, "Just call. Just like you used to." Then he looked up the road at the camper and Janine's trailer and asked if we wanted a ride. I told him no. He looked up the road again, like he wouldn't take no for an answer. But then he nodded, said "Let me know," and drove slowly away.

I know it doesn't make sense to be so scared of him. He has taken better care of Jade and me than anyone ever has. But sometimes, when I feel that current, that mind numbing current, it feels like I'm teetering on the edge of some abyss, or like some tidal wave is going to wash me away.

Ruby Jennings   8/2/1998

The days are so hot and long, and they're starting to run together. We have groceries in the little fridge for now. I stay inside during the high heat. I'm avoiding Janine as much as I'm avoiding the sun. Every time I go outside, I see those curtains move. I can't see her face, but I can feel her watching me. She wants me gone, but I don't have anywhere to go.

Sometimes, in the early mornings, I take Jade for walks in the fields behind the camper. There's this place I found, it's a circle of oak trees, five of them, and they're all growing outward from each other. In the middle it's shady and clear of cactus and cedar. It's so magical, I can almost imagine fairies in the shadows, floating in the filtered light between the branches. I take Jade there and spread a blanket out, and she plays with her baby dolls while I draw.

We stay there until the heat invades our little haven. And then I have to step out into the harsh sun and carry her back to the real world. Somewhere in the back of my mind, I hear that old shrieking panic, but it's muffled by something dark and heavy inside of me. It's a paralyzing mix of fear and exhaustion and hopelessness.

Dad finally comes back on Sunday night. This might be the first time I've ever waited for him. He's still driving that car. It's a blue-green Mitsubishi or something. I guess he finally bought one.

When he comes in, he looks right over me, at the bunk, and I know he came home to crash. I'm in his way though, and I have Momma's journal. I also have the board with her name carved into it sitting on the table. They've been sitting out since yesterday.

He looks me over, sizing me up, like he's wondering how much trouble I'm going to be. And I'm glad he knows by the look on my face that I want something. I won't have to figure out how to bring it up.

"What?" he asks. "What do you think you're gonna get out of me? What do you think it's gonna change?"

I think for a second about that. What do I think it's going to change? I don't know. Nothing he says can change the past. But I can't think too long, because I don't want to miss my chance. He's shuffling from foot to foot and adjusting his cap lower over his face. I get the feeling he's about to turn and leave again.

"I want to know if you ever cared about her," I say. "She was my mother, and I just want to know if you ever really loved her."

"Look, Jade," he says. I can't remember the last time he said my name. "I've done a lot of bad things. Things you never need to know about—"

"THAT'S NOT WHAT I'M ASKING!" I interrupt him before he can start with his excuses. I'm so frustrated and so tired of waiting for this answer, I scream at him. "DID YOU LOVE HER?"

"YES GODDAMMIT! I LOVED HER!" He screams back at me. And he's breathing hard, but he's not shuffling anymore. He has his hands down. They're fists at his sides. "I was trying! I know I didn't deserve her. But I was fucking trying!"

Dad is standing in front of me crying, and now I don't know what to do.

"You're right. I left her here. And I can't blame anyone else for what happened. Because I left her here. Is that what you want to hear? Are you happy now? Will that give you closure?" He's turning mean again, and he makes quotes in the air when he says "closure."

I don't feel like fighting anymore. I just whisper, "No."

"Then I don't know what you want," he says. "But I sure as hell don't have it."

He pulls his cap off, runs a hand through his feathery thin hair. He has sores on his face, around his mouth. He's shuffling again, rolling his head

227

back and forth with his words. "Every fucking day! Every fucking day, I live with this. And then I come home and there's you. Staring at me."

Then he lets out a howl and bangs the side of his hand on the cabinet over the sink.

"I can't even miss my mother like a normal person," I say, and I'm surprised by how calm I am. I flip the pages in the journal, back to the picture of us. The one taken at Sears. "Look at her," I say.

But I know he won't. He glares at the journal, glares at me. Then he says, "Fuck this shit," and walks back out the door.

I'm not mad anymore. I think I understand.

Ruby Jennings   8/7/1998

I woke up today and I got right up. I made myself do it. I got dressed, really dressed, not just that old cotton sun dress. I put on jeans and shoes. I got Jade dressed too. And I walked into town and went to the welfare office and started filling out forms. I used the address off the mailbox at the end of the road.

I don't know how I'll get my mail from Janine. But I'm guessing if she hasn't told me to leave yet, she probably isn't going to. And if she's going to let me stay, maybe she'll give me my mail too.

I reapplied for the Early Head Start program, and for food stamps and AFDC, all of it. I won't find out until right before school starts back if there's a spot for Jade at EHS. I might have to ask Rita to watch her. Maybe she won't mind if I give her half my food stamps.

I just wanted to write this down, how good it feels to get up with a reason and to get something done.

Ruby Jennings   8/10/1998

I can't believe I didn't go fill out those forms earlier. I don't know what we're going to eat. It could be two more weeks before I get my food stamps. I don't have any money for anything. I was thinking about asking Janine to borrow some money until my check comes in, but then I came back from a walk with Jade this morning, and I saw the electric bill slipped into the door of the camper. It's over a hundred dollars. Because of the air conditioner, I'm sure. So, I'm guessing she won't want to help.

I fed Jade the last two hot dogs. I still have a can of SpaghettiOs and two cans of beanie-weenies. So if I don't eat, we still have a few days.

I want to call Mrs. Patterson, but then I think about the last time we talked. I know she doesn't want to hear from me. I don't want to tell her what happened. She'll think she was right, and I'll have to pretend I learned my lesson. I'll have to pretend I'm not just holding on, waiting for Jimmy to get out.

Maybe I'll call Ellis.

School started today, and Jade has a spot in Early Head Start. Thank goodness. I don't think I'd make it through a day if I had to leave her at Rita's. Ellis picked us up at the end of the road and drove us. He's been around a lot lately. I haven't told Jimmy that. I didn't even want to write it down. Like I'm hiding it from myself or something. I don't know why.

I finally walked down to the convenience store and asked the lady behind the counter if I could borrow the phone. I was out of milk. I didn't have to say much. Just, "Ellis, I think I need some help." And then I kind of choked but I finally managed to say, "We're almost out of food."

He told me to stay there. He pulled into the parking lot less than twenty minutes later. First, he took us through the McDonald's drive-through. I ate my chicken nuggets, all twenty of them, so fast I was surprised when I got to the bottom of the box. I was sort of sad there weren't more. I didn't tell him I'd only eaten a couple of crackers in the last two days. I felt guilty about eating those when Jade could have had them.

Ellis took us to Brook's Brothers after that. We went through the aisles together, quiet and awkward like always. I told him over and over that I'd have my food stamps in a few days. I told him I didn't need much. But he piled things into the cart, until I told him my fridge was too small to hold any more.

Then he drove us back to the camper and helped me put the groceries away. So I told him I'd make some spaghetti, if he wanted to stay and eat with us.

I stood at the tiny stove, browning the hamburger meat, with this pain in my throat that I couldn't swallow away. I think the shame finally got to me. Being a beggar. Reduced to asking someone for help even when your entire soul is in revolt against it. It's harder to notice that kind of shame on an empty stomach.

<u>Ruby Jennings</u>   <u>9/2/1998</u>

Rita's fighting with her boyfriend worse than ever. I try to understand what they're fighting about. I don't get it. She started coming over to her mother's house a lot. I see her car parked there all day. Which is weird, because she never invites me and Jade over for these visits.

Sometimes Rita stops to see me when she's leaving. That's when I hear about how awful her boyfriend is, and how she's going to leave him. But nothing she complains about seems like a big deal to me. Or at least it's not a big deal if you love someone, like I love Jimmy. I don't know if Rita ever loved Clay. And whatever softness there was in Rita seems to be slipping away with every visit to her mother's house.

I live right beside my mother-in-law, on her property with her granddaughter. I know Jimmy talked to her about me. He said he called and asked if I could stay in the camper. She said we could. But she acts like she barely knows we're alive.

I don't know what I did wrong. I know it shouldn't hurt my feelings.

They're not my actual family, but they're the closest thing I have.

So now that school has started, I a reason to get up in the morning. And one more semester until I graduate. I feel almost normal again.

Mrs. Patterson called me to her office to see how things were going. I told her we're fine. I'm not sorry for marrying Jimmy. She wants me to just wipe him out of my life. And I don't want to hear it. So, I avoid her.

Ruby Jennings   9/6/1998

I feel like I'm buried inside myself when I'm around Ellis. He comes by every week to take us to the jail to see Jimmy. I can't really remember how it started. I guess he picked me up walking one day, and then he started getting to the camper before I could get out the door.

The second I get into the truck with him I can't think. My mind just hibernates. We barely speak to each other. I stare out the window or stare at my hands. We've done this so many times, you'd think I'd be used to him. He always has something for Jade when he comes. A toy, candy, something. When we get out, he always carries her inside.

Jimmy and Ellis talk about the trial and the lawyers and the judge and the setup and all the things that never had anything to do with me. Jimmy always thanks Ellis for taking care of us. And then, if Ellis gets up and leaves us alone long enough, Jimmy tells me how sorry he is. That he didn't mean to leave us. He was just trying to get ahead so he could make a new life for us. I tell him he doesn't have to be sorry. That I love him, and it will all be over soon. I keep telling him he'll be home soon. And I can tell by the way he looks when I say it, it's not true.

Ellis started taking us to the Granite Ridge Café to eat after we see Jimmy. We were walking out of the jail one day, and he asked if I was hungry. So now that's what we do. We go see Jimmy, and we go eat at the café, and he gets blueberry cream pie and feeds it to Jade.

Some of the customers might think we're a family. A giant tattooed brute with a skinny redheaded wife who barely talks and can't stop playing with her wedding ring. But the ladies that wait on us know who Ellis is. They know who Jimmy is too. I can't imagine what they think of me.

Ruby Jennings   10/3/1998

The trial started. I skipped school a couple of times to sit in the courtroom, but Jimmy keeps telling me I don't need to be there, that I don't need to know what happened. He says I need to be in school. So I try to go to school and wait until I can talk to him and find out how it's going. But a couple of days this week I just couldn't stand it. So, I went.

On Thursday, I sat down beside Ellis in the row of seats against the back wall. He looked up at me like he was mad that I was there, but I sat by him anyway. Rita and Janine were sitting right behind Jimmy in the front row. I wasn't about to sit by them. I didn't want everyone in the room to look up at me when I came in. Rita and Janine wouldn't want me beside them anyway.

The cop that led the investigation was in the wooden box beside the judge. I don't think he's the kind of cop to wear a uniform. He was wearing a polo shirt, but I knew he was a cop because of the way he talked. He kept saying the informant did this and the informant said that. And things like, "we received a tip from a concerned citizen that Mr. Jennings was planning something big," and increased surveillance. That's when I finally put it all together.

It was me. I told Mrs. Patterson that Jimmy was planning something big. Mrs. Patterson must have told the police. That's how they were able to set him up.

All of this is my fault.

❖ ❖ ❖

So that explains it. Mrs. Patterson kept my mother's journal from me all this time because that old busy body narced on my dad. She butted her nose into our lives, and she probably justified it in her own mind by thinking she was doing the right thing. Doing her job.

Her job. Our lives.

And Momma, my fragile desperate Momma, had to carry this burden by herself. The fear. She had to be so scared of what Uncle Ellis and Harmon would do, even what Dad might do, if they knew.

And of course, the guilt. Guilt that ruined any chance she ever had to be happy.

School starts tomorrow. I'll have to look at Mrs. Patterson. I'll have to look at the real reason my mother was "so sorry" for everything, all the time.

Mrs. Patterson must either be very smart, knowing I can't tell Dad what she did without telling him Momma's part in it. Or this woman is really stupid. Because if Uncle Ellis or Harmon found out what she did… If I were Mrs. Patterson, I would have burned this journal.

There aren't many pages left. I know the rest of this story. I don't have to read it. But I do anyway.

Ruby Jennings   10/9/1998

I got high with Carrie at the park today. I guess it isn't skipping school if you're old enough to sign yourself out. I don't know why I did it. I just wanted some peace.

I get busy during the day, and I sort of forget. But it's always there, ruining everything. Then, when I'm walking home, or when Jade falls asleep, it comes back to me. It washes over me all over again, that feeling that I don't deserve to be happy ever again. I press my eyes closed tight, but there's no escaping it. It's my fault.

I can't accept it, and I can't change it.

When I got high today, I floated away from everything for just a second. Just far enough so I could think without feeling.

I didn't even go back to class when Carrie did. I picked up Jade from Early Head Start instead. I told them I was sick and I was taking her home. They track my attendance. I'll get kicked out of the program if I miss too much school or she misses too much daycare. Oh well.

I took Jade home, and then we sat on our blanket in between the fairy trees, singing songs until the sun went down. She brought me leaves and flowers and patted my head. And when I closed my eyes, she kissed each eyelid, saying "mwah" each time.

Jimmy's gone. They sent him to a diagnostic unit, and now he's in a medium security prison in Gatesville. His truck was sold at an auction somewhere. And Jade and I are still here on this patch of land with her family, even though they don't really want me. I think Janine would be happiest if I left, but Rita says she doesn't want me to take Jade away.

Ruby Jennings   10/26/1998

I didn't go to school today. I finally bought my own bag of weed from Oliver and went home with it.

I'm tired of Carrie. Sometimes she talks so long and so pissed off, I find myself just staring at her, wondering when she'll ever shut up. Wondering how she can think anything matters. That anything is worth that much energy.

It all goes wrong.

I didn't want to sleep with Ellis. But what was I going to do? Say no? At first I didn't think it was that big of a deal, really. I was high as hell, but he didn't know that. I wasn't really paying attention to him, or I would have seen it coming and avoided it. But I was working on a sketch, when he came over. He was early to pick us up and take us to Gatesville. Jade was asleep.

Maybe he thought I wanted him to kiss me or something. I think I stood in the door too long. But really I just didn't know what to do about him being so early. And then it took me a second to realize what was happening. And then I just didn't know how to stop it. I didn't want to hurt his feelings or make him mad.

And I'm writing all of this down, trying to understand. I can't figure out how I could let this happen? Nothing will ever be the same. Even if Jimmy never finds out, Ellis and I will know. And now I know how easily Ellis will betray Jimmy. But then it wasn't much of a betrayal really, was it? I mean if I'm really this kind of a slut, then Ellis just did him a favor right?

Everything is ruined. Forever. No going back. Ruined.

And after we did that, I sat in the truck with him all the way to Gatesville, silent and sick to my stomach. And then we sat and talked to Jimmy, and I couldn't look at either of them. But Jimmy didn't notice anything different, he was just so happy to see us.

He gets more desperate every time we see him. Desperate to see us. Desperate to get out. He's gotten beat up a few times, and it scares me. He swears he's staying out of trouble so he can get out and get home. To us.

And not for one second have I been able to forget that it's my fault he's locked up in the first place.

Ruby Jennings   11/12/1998

Ellis hasn't been around for a few days, and I hope it's because he's as disgusted as I am by what we did. Maybe we really can just pretend it never happened. I keep telling myself it's not the same as causing Jimmy to go to Prison. Nothing bad has to come of this thing between me and Ellis, as long as Jimmy never knows.

But then I remember what I really did that was really bad, that Jimmy is paying for, even if he doesn't know it was me. And I wonder what difference any of it makes anyway.

Ruby Jennings   11/15/1998

I got some Xanax from Oliver because I knew Ellis would be back to take us to Gatesville on Saturday. Jimmy would think something was wrong if he didn't bring us. But Ellis waited in the truck for us instead of coming inside the camper. Then he tried to talk about it on the drive. Not outright. Just in a roundabout way. He just said he was sorry if he upset me last time. He said he had been trying to get some distance. Just generic guy talk that doesn't really mean anything specific. Just a slippery way of saying sorry and let's forget about it.

And I felt better. Much better.

But then he carried Jade into the camper when we got home.

This time, I didn't hate it. It was nothing like being with Jimmy. It was like I dissolved. Like I just dove into my fear of him, right into the fire, and burned all the way down. I disappeared. Finally.

CHAPTER 16

Colby and I are up and out of the house before Gina and the twins. I'm only ready to go back to school because I'm looking forward to hanging out with Jathan. And ready to be out of the camper. But I do not want to lay eyes on Mrs. Patterson.

I finished the journal last night.

I don't see Mrs. Patterson in the halls all morning. She doesn't call me into her office either. Colby is trying to remind me how he found his father because of the journal. And how she saved Colby from some serious trouble. And he also points out how Dad could have gotten himself arrested, even if she hadn't butted her nose in.

I won't let Colby read the journal. I told him the parts he needs to know. Aunt Rita and Grandma did enough talking about Momma and Uncle Ellis while Dad was locked up. Colby doesn't need any more proof that it was all true. After Dad got out, with Momma gone, they finally shut up about it. They just stopped talking about her altogether. Dad called Uncle Ellis, and everything went back to normal between them. Like Momma never existed.

It's after lunch when I see Mrs. Patterson. I'm sitting on the bench in my place in the sun. She sneaks up like she does and sits down beside me. I don't even jump this time. I just keep reading Rebecca, for my English class. And I know I'm not the same person I was just a few weeks ago. I know this because I didn't jump. Because I'm not scared of her. I don't care what she wants. And I am absolutely certain she is no one I can ever trust.

"I thought you might have stopped by to see me," she says.

"Why would you think that?" I turn the page on my book, even though I didn't finish reading it.

"I thought you might have questions for me? About the journal?"

"Nope," I say. "It's pretty simple stuff."

"I thought I might explain some things." She slides her hands down her thighs, smoothing her flowery broom skirt over her knees.

"Really?" I ask her. "You think you understand that journal better than I do?" I sound hateful.

She doesn't even look surprised. "I think there are some things in it that need explaining," she says.

"Really? Really, Mrs. Patterson? Because I think I understand it. I mean, after all, I lived it," I say, and my voice gets low. "Every single thing in that journal affected me. My life, Mrs. Patterson. Not yours."

"Jade," Mrs. Patterson says, "There are things I want to explain."

"No, let me explain, Mrs. Patterson. I'm not my mother. I don't need you." I stand up. I don't even bother putting my book in my bag before I walk away. "I think you've caused enough problems with your talking."

I guess I could get in trouble for being disrespectful. I sort of expect to get called to the principal's office, or maybe to her office, but I don't. The day ends like nothing happened.

Jathan and I walk home, and it feels good to be back to some kind of normal.

I'm extra respectful to Sheila. I want her to forget all about seeing Uncle Ellis at the park. I even carry out the trash and load the dishwasher. I feel better about the whole situation when she gives me a side hug and kisses me on top of the head. I mean, I'm weirded out by it, because I'm not used to hugging and kissing. But I feel like it's a good sign. Like she doesn't regret trusting me with Jathan.

She tries to get me to stay for dinner, and I tell her I have a ton of homework. And then she tries to get me to stay to do that too. Which is new. And she offers to drive me home. I'm starting to think she feels sorry for me since she saw where I live. I can't believe it took me so long to figure this out. I guess I thought all those busy bodies already told her how I live in a camper out in the sticks. I thought she knew. Oh well. It's embarrassing, but I guess her pity's better than her not wanting me around.

I'm not letting her drive me home. Heaven help me if Dad happened to be there when she drove up. He would probably do something embarrassing. Not to mention I don't want her to ever see where I live again.

When I get home, I go to Colby's room. I want to tell him what I said to Mrs. Patterson. I want to know if he thinks I'm going to be in trouble.

"I think if you were going to be in trouble, she would have called you out right there," he says.

"Can you believe her?" I ask him. "Can you just believe the nerve of her to want to talk about it?"

"You should hear what she has to say."

"Don't take her side," I tell him. "Just because she got you out of trouble. You could have figured out who your dad was by yourself. It doesn't make up for what she did to Dad."

I guess this makes Colby mad, because he says, "Oh, now your poor Dad is the victim of mean old Mrs. Patterson?"

"You know what I mean," I say.

"Nope, I don't know what you mean. Your dad is the reason your dad went to prison. And you've always known that. So, you get your dad to talk to you for five seconds about your mother, and now you need someone else to blame for what happened to her."

I glare at Colby. I'm not quite sure if I want to tell him off or storm out, so I just glare at him while I make up my mind.

"I don't need someone else to blame. But there *is* someone else to blame," I start rolling these words out. Words that I've been playing in my mind all

244

day. Words I prepared in advance to say to Mrs. Patterson. Or to anyone who ever judged my mother, like Aunt Rita and Grandma. But instead, I'm pouring them out on Colby. Dumping them on him. "My mother died believing she was the reason Dad was locked up. You don't know the things she did, the things she lived with. Things she couldn't live with…" And then I run out of gas because it's unbearable. It is still so unbearable. "I just want my mother back."

I put my face in my hands and wait for the stinging in my eyes to pass, for the knot in my throat to shrink. I'm grateful Colby lets me get it together instead of trying to hug me or something awkward like that.

"I know you do," is all he says.

But that doesn't really help me. It makes it feel like I'm being irrational. Wanting something I can't have and being mad at people who didn't do anything wrong.

Dad hasn't been home in almost a week and a half. That's a long time, even for him. I never really thought about what I'd do if he didn't come back. I mean I can call him on his cell. But what do I say? I'm worried about you? Then after the second week, I get the electric bill. That seems like a legitimate reason to call him. But he doesn't answer. So after a few more days, I give in and call Uncle Ellis.

I have to borrow Colby's cell phone, so Uncle Ellis wants to know why I don't have my own cell phone. And I don't want to get into that with him.

His little digs, telling me how Dad isn't good enough. I know he isn't. I don't need to hear it.

"I need to find Dad," I say.

"Why?" he asks. "What do you need?"

"Dad," I say.

"Don't get smart with me," he says. "I'll find your Dad. But I know you aren't calling because you miss him. So, what do you need?"

"I miss him."

"Since when?" he laughs.

It isn't the first time I've wondered how Uncle Ellis decides right from wrong. This is the man who took care of me when my mother was so messed up on pills she couldn't get out of bed. He played with me, read to me, taught me to ride a bike. He bought us groceries, cooked me dinner, walked me to class on my first day of kindergarten. And he loved my mother.

But he wasn't supposed to. He's my dad's best friend.

He has to know what that did to her. Even if he doesn't know everything.

"I need to pay the electric bill."

"I'll bring you some money," he says.

"Where's Dad?"

"I'll find him," he says.

It makes me even more nervous that Uncle Ellis doesn't know where Dad is. If anything happens to Dad, especially after I drug up all that history about Momma… I hang up the phone and wait. Because, as much as I hate him, as much as I wish it weren't true, Uncle Ellis is the one who has always taken care of things.

Colby has been to see his real dad a bunch of times. They meet for lunch on Saturdays. He met his other sister, which is weird to me. That he has a sister I'm not related to. She's my age, and I want to know what she's like. I wonder if she's anything like Colby. If she is, I think we could actually be friends.

Aunt Rita still doesn't know Colby found his dad. I keep asking Colby when he's going to tell her. I guess his dad, Allen, is asking him the same thing. So it seems now Allen has a thing about kids not lying to their parents. I don't even make a joke about that to Colby. It's really not funny.

Anyway, I'm not the only one with a dad who made mistakes. I mean, I guess it'd be easier to forgive a dad that drove a BMW and didn't actually go to prison. It'd probably be easier to forgive a dad who asked for forgiveness too. So, Colby is way ahead of me in that.

Uncle Ellis drug Dad home. With a broken arm. I think they got in a fight.

Uncle Ellis didn't have any marks on him, but I guess he wouldn't. I think they had a fight because of the way Dad kept yanking his good arm away from Uncle Ellis. Uncle Ellis was only trying to help him into the camper. I've never seen Dad get mad at Uncle Ellis before. That scared me. It was like watching one of those Spanish bull fights or something. Like something very bad could happen any second, but there's no way to tell what it will be or when.

But Uncle Ellis didn't lose his temper with Dad, which surprised me even more. Especially since I'm pretty sure he's the one who broke Dad's arm.

I sort of wish Uncle Ellis would have left Dad wherever he was. But I'm also worried Dad's going to go off and kill himself, whether he means to or not. He's the skinniest I've ever seen him, and he's popping pain pills for his arm, taking way more than he should. I'm doing my best to help him. But he's been home for four days, and I just want to get away from him.

The fight about Momma is hanging between us. I'm not mad at him anymore. That's a huge relief for me. But I think it's still bothering him. Not that he'd ever come out and say it. He's just taking it out on me.

He won't let me go anywhere except to school and to the Millers'. And he yells at me every time I make the slightest move. He acts like he's stuck in the camper with me, but as far as I can tell he could leave anytime he wanted to. Broken arm or not.

Unless he's here because Uncle Ellis broke his arm and told him to stay here. To take care of me.

CHAPTER 17

When Jathan and I get to the Millers' house after school on Monday, there's a stack of Home Depot boxes leaning against the arm of the couch. So I ask Jathan what they're for.

"We have to move," he says, and flops down on the couch while I stand there staring at him. He picks up his PSP and starts playing a game, chin tucked into his chest, shoes on the edge of the table, while the room closes in on me.

"Move?" I ask him. "Move where? Why?"

"My dad is getting transferred," he says, irritated and pouty.

"What?"

He heaves a big, defeated breath and shrugs, "I know," he says. "Totally sucks."

"But what about…" I start to ask, but I don't even know where to start. I sit down beside him and look around the room. The nick-nacks are all gone from the shelves beside the TV. The cords are wrapped around the bases of the lamps on the end tables. The picture frames are all stacked in a Home Depot box by the entrance to the hall.

"Where?" I finally ask. Maybe it won't be that far. Maybe I can get a real job and a car.

"Some place called Richardson," he says without looking up from his game. "I think it's by Dallas."

Too far for me to drive.

I forget to make him do his homework. I forget to make him a snack. He sits beside me and plays his PSP until Sheila comes home. She's mad when she sees us.

"Jathan, you were supposed to be packing up your room," she tells him. She puts her keys in her purse and swings it down from her shoulder into the chair by the door.

I know she's about to ask him what we've been doing this whole time. Why we haven't gotten anything done. But when she looks at me, she doesn't say anything.

"Oh honey, I'm so sorry," she starts. "I should have told you, but we weren't sure until late Friday night. There wasn't a good opportunity."

"No," I say, "that's fine. Really, I understand." But really it's not fine. Not fine at all. And I'm trying hard not to cry. And I hate Sheila now more than ever. "When will it be?" I ask.

"Probably the end of next week," she says. "We have a ton to get done before then."

I nod my head a little. It's all I can manage. I think I should be offering to help pack or something like I normally do, to make sure she likes me. But I can't bring myself to do it. I don't want this. This can't happen. I won't offer to help make it happen faster.

I get my book bag and my coat and walk out the door. I say bye, or something like it. Sheila keeps trying to talk to me and ask questions, but I just can't really understand her, or I can't listen. My ears are ringing, and I just need her to stop talking.

I walk home, and I'm hoping some idea is going to come to me. Some way to fix this. To stop this. But there's nothing. I can't do anything. I can't say anything. To anyone.

And then I'm home, and there's Dad in the camper. And I'm trapped with him. He's drifting in and out of sleep, from whatever pain meds he's taking. He keeps asking me for water, but he still has the first glass I gave him on the window ledge by his head.

In my mind I'm trying to make a list of people who could possibly help me. But there's no one on that list. I can't go to sleep. I can't talk to Colby on the way to school. I can't concentrate in class.

I don't know what comes over me after lunch. I kind of expect her to find me. I guess I think she has some magic connection to me, that she would know how bad this is. But she doesn't come. Maybe she really gave up on me. I don't go to my next class. I go to her office.

And she has someone in there with her, so I have to wait by Mrs. Perkowski, who smiles at me even while she hates me. And I'm mad that I have to wait, because this is an emergency. There's nothing else that would bring me back into this office to talk to that woman, except an absolute emergency.

And finally, the kid that has been talking to Mrs. Patterson comes out with a yellow slip of paper on top of her new schedule. And Mrs. Perkowski smiles at her and tells her to have a good day. And I realize I probably look like I'm snarling at Mrs. Perkowski, because of the way I'm chewing the side of my bottom lip while I listen to her talk to this other girl.

Finally, Mrs. Patterson comes out and looks like she's on her way out of the office when she sees me. I'm afraid she's going to tell me she has a meeting or something and I need to come back. But she doesn't.

She stops like someone pulled an invisible string on her back and then says, "Jade, I didn't realize you were waiting. Come on in."

I follow her back into her office and sit down. She's there across the desk from me, waiting to see what I want. And it's me that wants something. I came here. So, it's on me to talk.

I open my mouth a few times. Trying to figure out how to break the logjam that has been in my mind for the last eight years. Where will I start?

"Mrs. Patterson, I need help," I say, then I'm stuck again.

"How can I help you Jade," she asks, so professional I wonder if I'm making a huge mistake. She has a pen in her hand. She's turning the lid, pulling it off, putting it back on, then turning it again.

I think about getting up and leaving. I think I'm going to throw up. But I can't forget the most important thing. So I just say it.

"Mrs. Patterson, Jathan Miller is my little brother, and he's about to move way up by Dallas, and I may never see him again."

She looks like she didn't really understand what I said. Like she wanted me to repeat it. But I can't. She sits there, and I can see her mind working, but I don't know what it could be working on. Mrs. Patterson has no idea what happened after Momma finally dropped out of school.

"Jade," she says after a few tries, "I need you to start over. Jathan? What makes you think he's your brother?"

And I guess she might think Dad had some kid with some other woman or something. So I start over.

I go all the way back, and I tell her about Momma and Uncle Ellis. How Uncle Ellis took care of us when Dad was locked up. How he was like my dad. How I never knew any different. I couldn't remember anything else.

And how Momma was so sad about him, even though he took care of everything, even me. How he'd get me dressed and take me to school. And bring groceries. And I didn't really understand why Momma didn't like him, but she was nice to him all the same. She did what he said.

Sometimes he'd yell at her to get up and get herself together. And she would. She'd cry and say she was sorry. But she'd take a shower and get dressed and she'd try. Those were the times that she would work in the garden, and we'd play and go for walks, and she was my magical Momma again.

Uncle Ellis used to ask her all the time to come and live with him. To get us out of the camper, away from Aunt Rita and Grandma. But she always told him they were my family. And she never had her family, so she wanted me to have mine. And she'd say she belonged to Dad. Except she'd say, "I belong to Jimmy." And then she'd get sad all over again.

And I don't know how it got so mixed up. I was only six, but I couldn't tell if Momma wanted Uncle Ellis to stay or go. She was sad no matter what he did. I wasn't sure we'd be okay if he went away for good.

I'm telling Mrs. Patterson these things, and she doesn't look surprised. She looks sad. And I realize that everyone knew about Uncle Ellis and Momma. Even if they never read the journal. None of this is a surprise to her at all. She still can't understand what I'm trying to say.

So then I tell her about how Aunt Rita started asking Momma about Uncle Ellis. Why he was always around? Did Jimmy know he was taking me and Momma places? Did Momma worry about breaking Dad's heart when he heard the rumors that his wife was betraying him with his best friend?

Momma told Uncle Ellis about Rita's questions. And Uncle Ellis told Momma she should move in with him. Back then I didn't really know why she couldn't. I guess now I understand. Because she thought it was her fault Dad went to prison in the first place. But more than that. She really didn't want to break Dad's heart. Because Aunt Rita was right. They were betraying him.

And sometimes Momma and Uncle Ellis would get into fights. I remember Uncle Ellis holding her down on the bed once when I was about four. But I was glad he did. She had a razor blade, and she was going to cut herself. And he asked her what she thought would happen to me if she did that. I think about him saying that. All the time. I think about how much more time I had with Momma because he was there. And I hate him because I think she's gone because he was there.

Uncle Ellis always held her until she calmed down, then she begged him not to leave her until she fell asleep.

Mrs. Patterson is watching me while I'm explaining all of this. And she looks sad. But confused.

And so, I tell her about the test Momma bought. How it was so weird that Momma just seemed to clear up. Like a foggy day that just cleared. It was summertime, and I was out of school. She woke up and got dressed and even picked out my clothes for me. It was funny for her to pick out my clothes. Like all of a sudden I needed her to do that again.

We walked into town, and we went to the drugstore. Not the one in K-Mart where everyone went. But the one over by the Methodist church, where the old people go. She acted really nervous while she went up and down the aisles. That old lady, with the widest rear-end I've ever seen, kept coming up and asking if she could help Momma find anything. Momma must have looked like she was a cancer patient or something, so pale and skinny with dark circles under her eyes.

But Momma told her no. When Momma found what she was looking for, she held it close to her and covered as much of it as she could with her hands. She didn't even look at the man behind the counter while he rang her up. When he saw what she had, he stopped asking questions too. Like if she needed that test, she surely didn't need any lip balm or hand lotion.

When we got home, Momma went into the bathroom with that box. And when she came out, she was still. Not still in the normal way. But sort of still in her mind. Or behind her eyes. Calm. I thought it was good.

But it wasn't.

She stayed that way for a long time. She slept a lot, but she didn't take pills. She didn't smoke anything. She didn't drink. I was just a little kid, but I remember how I wasn't so nervous when she wasn't so skinny.

She was nice to Uncle Ellis. She stopped fighting with him. And he was happy. He bought her things and gave her all kinds of money. And she always acted like she didn't have any money, but I knew she had a bag of it. She kept it under the bench cushion.

School started again. Then one morning, we left for school, but we didn't actually go to the school. She brought the bag of money with her that day.

She took my school papers and folders out of my backpack and stuffed it full of clothes. She had a big purse with her stuff in it. And we went to the Greyhound station, and we got on a bus.

I didn't even ask where we were going. Not because I didn't understand that leaving was bad. But I was afraid she would leave me behind if I asked too many questions.

By this time, I think Mrs. Patterson is starting to understand. It must have been the part about the test that made her understand. She looks like she's waiting for me to stop talking. I guess now she can think of some questions. I'm getting to the hard part. I don't think I want to talk anymore anyway.

"Your mother was pregnant?" Mrs. Patterson says. She has taken the words from my five-year-old mind and turned them into the adult facts.

I don't move. Surely, she doesn't expect an answer to the obvious.

Instead, I tell her about living in the motel with Momma while her belly got so big I couldn't sit on her lap anymore. About how we played Barbies, and paper-dolls and Candy Land on the extra bed. How I slept with her every night, with no idea anything was wrong.

I told her how Momma had our baby. We went to the hospital in a cab, and I waited out in the hallway where the nurses called my Momma indigent. I looked it up later. I guess it was true.

We brought him back to the motel. He was like a baby doll. I took care of him. I changed his diapers and gave him his bottle, and I saved his umbilical cord. I still have it. He was all red and wrinkly, but he got fatter, and he was starting to smile, even though Momma said it was probably just gas.

But then, Darcy, the lady that took our rent money, started getting mad at Momma. Momma tried to keep her from knowing when we came and went. But then Darcy left a note on the door telling Momma that she was going to change the lock, and we had two days to get our stuff out.

So Momma sold some of our stuff, and we got back on the Greyhound bus. We got to Oak Grove in the middle of the night, and Momma rented another room. But she didn't let me go to sleep.

Our baby was named Jacob then. She told me to take him in his car seat to the fire station. It was almost March, so it was still kind of chilly at night. And I sat him there under the light where the moths were flying around. I waited in the park, in the tunnel slide, for someone to come outside and find him. He was quiet at first. Then he woke up and started crying. That was when the door opened.

I hid there and watched them take him inside. Then, later someone carried him out to one of the normal sized trucks in the parking lot. They took forever to strap his seat in. I remember thinking it wasn't a fireman who took him, because the guy who drove was wearing jeans and a t-shirt. I thought that was strange back then. But later I figured out that firemen don't always wear those hats and coats.

Then I went back to the motel and slept with Momma, and I slept through the night for the first time since the baby was born. Jacob. Jathan. The fire station baby. The baby the Millers adopted.

We left again the next morning. To another place I'd never been, to another motel, where Momma spent the last of her money to pay for that one night. She told me to take care of him. She told me I'd get back to Oak Grove. Back to Jacob. That I had to watch out for him. She said she couldn't live without her baby, but she wouldn't let Uncle Ellis have him.

Then, right before I fell asleep, she was playing with my hair. She said, "You are so much stronger than I ever was."

"And when I woke up…" I cannot finish this, but I don't have to. These are the events everyone knows. What no one knows is how long I sat there, crying at my mother's feet. How long I begged her to wake up. How I didn't want to go for help because I knew that would make it final. Whoever came would do what grownups do. Clean things up and take things away.

But I didn't have to get help. The motel clerk, an older man, nothing like Darcy, came to check on us when he heard me crying for my Momma. I guess I was that loud.

CHAPTER 18

Mrs. Patterson is sitting at her desk looking at me. She looks like she wants to cry, but she can't get past the... what? Surprise? Shock? Disgust? I can't tell. I wish I could tell. I wish I knew what she was going to do. Because she could really mess things up for me. For everyone, Jathan, Sheila, everyone. I just want her to fix it, like she did for Colby. But I'm starting to worry now that there's no way she can.

I don't know how much time has passed. I'm shaking, and this seems like something I should be able to control, but I can't.

Finally, she speaks. Her voice starts out all croaky, but it clears up finally, and I'm able to figure out what she wants to know, "She was here in Oak Grove, and all she needed was money?"

I realize Mrs. Patterson is trying to figure out how this could be fixed, how she could have stopped it. I know this because I've wondered the same thing every day for the last eight years. But I also know that all kinds of things could have been different before Dad went to prison before Uncle Ellis... before Momma got pregnant. But not after.

"No," I say, "Momma knew what she was going to do as soon as she took that test from the pharmacy. She wanted me to be with my family. She wanted me to look out for Jathan. But she didn't want anyone to know he was Ellis' son."

Mrs. Patterson has this look on her face like she wants to argue with me, like it's up to me to change my mind about all of this. As if I can somehow put everything back together. But it's not up to me, and I can't fix it. I'm hoping she won't tell me all the things Momma could have done differently. Because defending my mother's decisions is not something I can do. She left me with the Jennings. She saved Jathan and left me to Dad because of some delusion she had that Dad was better than Uncle Ellis. That I had a family to take care of me.

I don't want to be pissed at my mother. I love her and miss her and want her back so bad it feels like a raw scream trapped in my lungs. But I can't help it, I'm mad as hell that she left me here.

Finally, Mrs. Patterson gets to the thing that hasn't happened yet. The thing that might still be fixed. "Jade," she says, "There are all kinds of legalities around adoption and child abandonment that —"

I start to get up. I should have known this was a mistake. I should have known she'd only make matters worse. If she opens her big mouth, if Uncle Ellis ever finds out about Jathan, the legalities are last thing we'll have to worry about.

"Wait, Jade," she puts her hand up, like she's pushing me back into the chair. "What I'm saying is that I don't think there is any way I can stop them from moving. In a situation like this, a child's father might have a custody case, but obviously that isn't a door we want to open."

I relax a little. Maybe she actually gets it.

"I don't know, Jade," she takes her glasses off and rubs the crease between her eyes. "I don't know."

We sit there for a while, and I think about my mother in this office, writing in her journal. This woman taking so much time with my mother, and with me, all those years ago. She must feel like we're close, but to me she still feels like a stranger.

I wait for her to think of something.

"Go back to class. Let me think this over," she says.

"Promise me you won't do anything without telling me first," I say.

"Jade, I did not turn your father in to the police," she says. "I need you to know that."

I don't have time to decide whether or not I believe her right now. "Promise me," I say again.

"I promise."

Two days go by with me helping Jathan pack more stuff from his room. I help Sheila dust and vacuum. I stay for dinner when she asks, because there's a real possibility this is the last time I'll have with him.

I'm waiting for Mrs. Patterson to call me to her office. I keep thinking about how hopeless it seemed for Colby, and what a miracle it was when she saved him. Any minute, maybe I'll get my miracle too.

So today at lunch, Mrs. Patterson is standing by the doors, waiting for me, when I come through. I'm as scared as I am hopeful. Surely this means she figured something out. She goes over to my usual bench, and I go with her even though I haven't gotten my lunch yet. She sits down, so I sit down and wonder how bad this is going to be.

"I'm going to talk to Mr. and Mrs. Miller," she says. "I'm going to explain the situation."

I could have done that myself. I've thought of that a thousand times. This is not the miracle I was looking for.

Mrs. Patterson is still talking, "They must think very highly of you. As his parents, they really are the only chance you have of maintaining a relationship with him."

"So, you're just going to ask them not to move?"

"I'd say it's unlikely they can change their career plans," she says. She's gripping her knees with her knobby old lady fingers. "You have to think they may be more motivated to move once they learn more about the situation," she says, kind of wincing like she expects me to get mad. "Not because of you, of course, but because of the other circumstances surrounding the adoption."

"Because of Uncle Ellis," I say, "Of course they'll want to leave when they know all that. They'll want to run further away than Dallas once they know all that. If they're smart."

She is watching me, and I figure out that she's asking me if it's okay. She wants my permission to tell Sheila. "So you're going to tell them all of this, and they're going to leave anyway." Maybe I get mad at her because it's better than crying. It really isn't her fault, exactly.

"It's my hope that the Millers will appreciate how much you care for their son, and work with me to help you maintain a relationship with him," she says. "I'll take you to see him as often as you like, if they'll allow it."

Now I feel like crying, and not because it sucks I won't be able to see him every day. Christmas break felt like a lifetime and all, but I feel like crying because I can't believe she'd go to that much trouble for me and my little brother. I can't believe anyone would.

I nod once. I have my teeth clenched. I don't look at her. I don't want to cry out here in the courtyard at school. She pats my back then gets up and leaves me there.

Then I get a note from Mrs. Patterson in my last period class. She has an appointment with Sheila tomorrow morning. That means I have one last afternoon with Jathan before everything changes.

Sheila notices that I'm sad. On my way out the door, she asks me if I'm okay. I don't even make up a lie. I just tell her I'm sad they're leaving. Then I walk home.

Dad is gone again. I guess that's not really a bad thing.

I get called to Mrs. Patterson's office in third period. I don't really trust my legs to carry me there, I'm so nervous.

Mrs. Patterson closes the door behind me, and I look through the glass at Mrs. Perkowski. Officer Perkowski's wife. Her flip-flops in the grocery store. Rita yelling at her. The dimples in the backs of her thighs, her beige shorts. It's a little tug, the connection. I wonder how much she can hear through Mrs. Patterson's office door.

I push that thought aside and look at Mrs. Patterson. I can't read her face.

She sits down at her desk and motions me to my regular chair. I don't imagine we'd need to take our places before starting if this was good news.

"I spoke with Mrs. Miller today," she starts, so formal. "You can imagine all of this is very difficult for her to process." She pauses.

I don't answer. I just want to know how it turned out.

"She's upset. Understandably," she says. "Alarmed, might be a better description. She feels very betrayed."

"What? What did you tell her? Betrayed? You must have told her something that's not true!"

"Jade, please try to understand where she's coming from. You've kept a very big secret for a very long time. A secret that could have very big implications to her family. To Jathan."

"No shit," I say, and I just know I'm going to get in trouble. "That's why I kept it a secret. She should know by now that she can trust me. I kept this secret for her family. For Jathan."

"She called Mr. Miller, and he came over to her office to visit with me as well," she goes on like I didn't just cuss in her office. "They feel like it would be best if they pick Jathan up from school until they're relocated to Richardson."

"So, I can't even see him again," I ask. "Is that what she means? I can't even say goodbye?"

She doesn't answer me, and it pisses me off even more. She knows how shitty this is. So shitty she can't even say, yes, they won't let you say goodbye to your little brother.

"Well, if you talk to her again, you tell her, you hear me? You tell her! You tell her I loved him first! I loved him longest. I love him most. He is my BLOOD! My mother's son. He looks just like my mother. And you tell that stupid cow I fucking hate her!"

I slam the door on my way out. Then I go to the bathroom, lock myself in a stall and fight the urge to leave school. I don't know how I'll go sit in a desk for the rest of the day, but I don't have anywhere else to go.

I walk home from school with Colby now. He knows I'm sad about Jathan leaving, even if he doesn't know exactly why. He leaves me alone about it. He lets me go into the camper without trying to follow me. And I sit by myself, fighting hopelessness, so afraid to end up like my mother. I have too much time to think.

I'm not mad at Mrs. Patterson. Not even mad at Dad anymore. I've spent a lot of time being mad at a lot of people. I guess it's one kind of motivation, being mad. Having someone to look out for is another.

I decide to be relieved that Jathan is out of Oak Grove. It's simpler this way. He doesn't really need me.

It's hard to rethink Momma. It's hard to admit that Sheila's a better mother for Jathan than Momma would have been. It feels like I'm being disloyal. But I have to figure out where Momma ended, and her depression began. It has to be possible to see the world for its art and beauty without sliding into the abyss. To be strong and not be hard. I have to figure this out.

I haven't told Colby about Jathan. Mrs. Patterson is the only person in Oak Grove who knows, and I feel sorry that I put that on her. She tells me I need to focus on school. That once I'm grown and Jathan is grown, we'll be able to have whatever relationship we'd like. That I can tell him anything I want about our mother.

She says this like it isn't ten years away from happening. I have a lot of time to kill. But at least I know he'll be okay.

It's the first day back after Spring break and Mrs. Patterson calls me to her office. She has a letter for me from Jathan. I know what this means. Jathan wanted to write to me, and Sheila couldn't give him any reason not to. I don't care. I'm just grateful.

Mrs. Patterson is looking at me like she wants me to open the letter in front of her. But I want to wait. I hold the envelope to my chest and tell her that I want to be alone when I read it. She says she understands and sends me back to class.

When I get home, I pull the envelope out of my book bag and peel open the flap, being careful not to tear it. His handwriting is terrible, and that makes me laugh. I guess they quit teaching cursive because he printed everything. He makes his p's funny. Just one single stroke, starting at the bottom then circling over to the right. I should have taught him to do it the right way. I would have.

He went to camp for Spring break. They made him write letters every day. He wrote this one to me on Wednesday. He wrote all about his new school and new friends. And he wrote about camp, how he hated craft time, but he was the best shot in archery, and he loved swimming. And he said he missed me because he had to go to an after-school program instead of walking home like he did in Oak Grove.

This is all good, I think.

I pull out some notebook paper and start my letter back to him. I tell him I miss him because I can't rub his cowlick anymore, and I don't have any video games to play, and no one tells me about good fantasy books. I draw a picture on the back of my letter. It's a sketch of him from my memory. He's sitting at his desk in his room, and he has the heel of his hand pressed into his forehead, his elbow on the desktop. He's reading a book.

I take the letter to Mrs. Patterson's office, and she gives me an envelope and a stamp. And then she hugs me on my way out the door. I let her. I let myself feel like I belong with her. Like we're close. I suppose we are.

I don't say anything, but she must know I love her for loving my mother.

ABOUT THE AUTHOR

Shannon Stewart is the mother of two very accomplished children, enjoys a rewarding career in technology, and spends her days with two wonderful canine companions.

www.ingramcontent.com/pod-product-compliance
Lightning Source LLC
Chambersburg PA
CBHW060306260626
47160CB00007B/2520